MURDER ON THE GOLF COURSE

An addictive crime mystery full of twists

ROY LEWIS

Arnold Landon Mysteries Book 14

Originally published as
The Ghost Dancers

Revised edition 2022
Joffe Books, London
www.joffebooks.com

First published in Great Britain in 1998
as *The Ghost Dancers*

ISBN: 978-1-80405-219-8

PROLOGUE

The Old King was dying.

He had been a great warrior chieftain. He had brought his people out of the marshes where the air was poisonous and the darkness of dreams filled with evil, peopled with whistling snakes that brought terror and death to all who were touched by them. He had led the way out of the swampland a generation ago and they had fought through the woods to the high ground overlooking the valley and there they had prospered, enslaving the people of the valley, holding back intruders, worshipping the sun and the moon and the gods that ruled their lives. He had ruled by terror and wisdom, violence and patronage, and those in his shadow had grown strong and prosperous. His sword and his spear cast a shadow over the high lands and none dared oppose him.

None but the shamans, and their opposition was not in the ways of men. They were the advisers who guided his life and guarded his spirit. To them, he listened in the darkness and heard of the gods who ruled their lives — of the manifestations and forms that they took, of the sacrifices they demanded, the blood, the death, the ritual that would ensure that he would live, and die, and come again to rule his people.

1

It was the gods who decreed that while he should have many wives he should have no sons. The shamans decreed that the male issue of his body should be strangled at birth, their bodies laid out on the hill. There the wolves might take their flesh and release their spirits to wander powerless, their strength dissipated, ethereal and weak, casting no shadows over him. And the shamans advised him also that it was well as he grew older that he put the older wives from him, that they became his 'sisters' and no longer had access to him, while the youngest and most beautiful of the women were ritually brought to him at the turn of the year, so that he might purify and strengthen himself in their bodies.

He was all-powerful, but he was old, and he was dying. The campaign to the coast had proved to be his last. There had been a revolt in the lands near the sea lagoon, which had spread across the hills, fuelled by the presence of a new man with a presence accustomed to command, a tall, strong man whose hair shone like burnished gold. Some said he came from beyond the seas, some said he possessed powers of witchcraft and could conjure wild-taloned birds to his aid, but whatever magnetized men towards him was powerful enough to make them die in his cause.

And they had died.

They had died in the swamps and the marshes, and they had died on the hills as the Old King had marched his cohorts to the boundaries of his people. They had fought madly under the leadership of the bright-haired man — but they had died.

It had been an unequal contest, for the Old King was war-wise. He had called together his warriors and they had gone down into the valleys to destroy the supply routes of the man with hair of gold. The tumult had been great. The woods had clashed to the sound of battle and great fires had been set in the villages, crops burned, the land laid waste. The Old King had rampaged wide, towards the sea lagoon, gradually increasing his stranglehold upon the opposing forces, seeking to extirpate all stains of the young man's support. It had been a slow and methodical progress and the campaign had lengthened into many months. The final battle had been fought on the shores of the lagoon and when it was over the shore had been red with blood, but the man with shining hair had breathed his last. He had come for conquest, yet had tasted death.

But when it was over, and he had conquered and the enemy was dead and his followers scattered, the old man was exhausted by the effort. His right arm had been broken by the blow of a dub, and he had experienced a crushing injury to his chest. When he breathed, deep, blood-stained spittle appeared on his beard, and his face was riven with agony.

After the battle was over, they stayed near the edge of the sea lagoon while the spirit-cleansing took place, and the death rituals were completed on the execution field. Only then, after two moons, did his captains bring him back to the hill. There, the shamans had been consulted and they had begun their spirit dance. Through the long twilight and the darkness of night they had shuffled and moved, twisting, gyrating, casting their runes, sending sparks and flames roaring to the heavens with the mysterious dust they cast into the ritual fire.

They danced, calling to the gods of the air and the darkness, seeking guidance from the ghosts of their past to ease the passage of the Old King to the underworld. For it was there that he would dwell, until he came again. The gods of the sky — eagle, boar, horse and stag — would release him from his earthly bondage, allow his reception deep in the bowels of the earth, where he would be regenerated like the seeds that grew to lusty life in the spring. They shuffled in their spirit dance, their ghost dance, calling up the souls of those who had gone before, demanding the release of the Old King from his dying flesh, seeking their guardianship through the tunnels and halls of the underworld, prophesying that he would come again, and lead his people once more.

They shuffled, and sang, and the sun rose upon them, and the Old King was dying . . .

CHAPTER ONE

1

The sub-committee met in the offices of the Leader of the Council. Most of the committee rooms seemed to have been commandeered already, but Arnold Landon had no objection to that if it meant they could take advantage of the rather more luxurious furnishings of the leader's office. The long boardroom table was flanked with well-upholstered chairs in an elegant blue, notepads had been neatly placed in front of each chair, bottles of spring water had been placed strategically along the table and there was also a sideboard with a drinks cabinet, though Arnold guessed that facility would probably not be available to them.

He was not a member of the committee, of course — Simon Brent-Ellis, the Director of the Department of Museums and Antiquities had that honour, but since he never moved far without support he had invited both his deputy, Karen Stannard, and Arnold to be in attendance. It was not that Brent-Ellis lacked the knowledge to play an adequate part in the discussions. It was simply that he felt the best way to avoid trouble was to have his minions with him, when decisions were being made. In that way, he could always blame them if things went wrong.

The three from the department were in fact the first to arrive. Surprisingly, in the case of Brent-Ellis, since he was not noted for his punctuality. Arnold guessed that his early presence today was due to the fact that his wife — the formidable Councillor Eleanor Brent-Ellis — was also a member of the committee.

She entered a little while after the departmental group, stocky, assertive, dark-browed and solid in build. She gave a nod to her husband, a wintry smile to Karen Stannard — whom she could not forgive for being beautiful — and affected to ignore Arnold. It was standard procedure as far as he was concerned. He had the impression he puzzled her. She was unable to weigh him up in her own mind, not certain whether he was a supporter of her husband, an enemy — or a buffoon. For his part, Arnold had a fairly clear view about her. He considered her to be a middle-aged termagant who terrified her husband, with her efficiency, her aggressiveness, and her cold, menacing eye.

The others trooped in a little while later: Councillor Tremain, chairman of the finance committee and a man who enjoyed power; the largely self-effacing Councillor Selkirk, Chairman of the Development Committee, and Councillor Tom Patrick, delegated to take the chair of this sub-committee to consider the undertaking known as the Stangrove Project.

Arnold observed Tom Patrick with some interest. He had had no dealings with the man but had heard a great deal about him. Tom Patrick had for some years run a highly successful training business in the north and had been elected to the council a year ago after some considerable scandals had rocked the council — there had been two prosecutions for bribery in respect of a road-widening project, and the councillor who had promoted the scheme had been forced out of office. Though new to politics, Tom Patrick had been elected after a vigorous *Clean Out Corruption* campaign, in which he had stressed that as a successful businessman he had no need to soil his hands.

He was about forty-five years of age, Arnold guessed, tall, well-built and smartly dressed in a dark suit, pale-blue shirt and subdued tie. There was an air of military precision about him, reflected in the neatness of his hair — which was dark but greying at the temples — the regulation inch of cuff he showed, and the manner in which he arranged the papers in front of him, squaring them off, shuffling them into place. He had heavy eyebrows, and his glance was sharp as he looked around the gathering. His mouth was firm and his jaw determined. Yet Arnold seemed to detect a certain theatricality about the man, as though he was playing a part. But perhaps all men holding public office held up a mask — of efficiency, of false bonhomie, of rectitude — or easy-going friendliness. With Tom Patrick, it was control.

'Thank you for your attendance, ladies and gentlemen,' he began, glancing around, his eyes lingering briefly but appreciatively on Karen Stannard. 'As you know, we're here today to consider the future of the Stangrove Project. While some of us are pretty up-to-date with what's being going on up at Stangrove, I believe the two main committee chairmen may not be completely familiar with its detail. It would be useful, therefore, if perhaps Mr Brent-Ellis could sketch in what it's all about.'

'Certainly, Chairman,' Brent-Ellis acquiesced, tugging nervously at the floral tie he wore, in stark contrast to the cream waistcoat and pale-blue suit he had affected on this occasion. He was always, Arnold thought resignedly, a flamboyant dresser, much to the annoyance of Chief Executive Powell Frinton who — had he been here — would have frowned his disapproval. 'The Stangrove Project is actually a development project that was instigated by the University of York. They set up a research team here in Northumberland some two years ago, to undertake investigation of an archaeological site in the North Tyne valley. My department was not involved since the work was being undertaken on a private site and no invitations were extended to seek our . . . ah . . . . assistance.' He wrinkled his nose in disapproval. Arnold suspected it was for the benefit of his wife, because the director was not notable for seeking extra work — for himself or his department. 'It seems that the university team was fairly successful in their mapping processes but then hit financial problems. Cutbacks at the university have meant that they are unable to proceed with the investigations; consequently, they have made an approach to our department with a view to ascertaining whether or not funding might possibly be forthcoming from this authority.'

'Fat chance,' Councillor Tremain rumbled. 'The way we're strapped for cash . . .'

'Quite so,' Brent-Ellis replied nervously, recognizing an opponent when he saw one. 'However, we were able to lend some assistance with a field team, and Miss Stannard has made some preliminary investigations. I think it would be appropriate, therefore, Mr Chairman, if we were to ask Miss Stannard to give her views about the project as a whole.'

Everyone looked at Karen Stannard.

The men did so eagerly, Mrs Brent-Ellis with reluctance.

Karen Stannard was wearing a dark-grey business suit that seemed to mould to her body, and the skirt was short enough to reveal her long, slim legs to advantage. She had recently returned to work from leave and her skin was tanned and light streaks had appeared in her hair, which she had left to grow a little longer. Though it was now tied back in a rather severe manner, it nevertheless seemed to enhance her femininity and the net effect was to showcase the classical line of her cheekbones and emphasize the beauty of her eyes. Arnold had never managed to decide what colour her eyes were. They seemed to change with her mood, and he had often enough seen them darken with anger. This morning her glance was confident and assured, and the colour was — he guessed — green. He shook his head resignedly. He still couldn't be sure.

'I've spent several days on site,' Karen Stannard was saying, 'and had the opportunity to discuss it in some detail with Mr George Pym, who is the site director, and his assistant

Miss Sue Lawrence. I should explain that the area is part of an old quarry site. It's not exactly a new archaeological find, in that aerial photographs taken in the nineteen-thirties identified the presence of rectangular enclosures. No excavations took place at that time and in the nineteen-sixties planning permission was given for gravel extraction — this work went on for some years, but fortunately it did not impinge too severely on the rectangles.' She paused, sweeping the listeners with her glance. 'Some damage has occurred, nevertheless, so it was fortunate that the land was acquired some five years ago by a wealthy businessman who brought the gravel extraction to a halt, and later issued an invitation to the university to undertake an investigation.'

As chairman of the finance committee, Councillor Tremain never understood why people gave up opportunities for profit. Suspiciously, he asked, 'Who is this philanthropist?'

Karen Stannard smiled. Her smile could be devastating. 'His name is Alan Farmer. I met him on site. He is semi-retired — wishes to live the life of a country gentleman, it seems. He made a fortune in developing computer software and now is more interested in quality of life, rather than making money.'

'So if that's his outlook, why doesn't *he* put money into this project, with the university strapped for cash?' Councillor Selkirk asked.

'He's already done so,' Karen Stannard replied, switching her smile in his direction to his obvious pleasure. 'But it was a balanced amount — set against the university's own commitment to the project. He's a great believer in self-help — an advocate of Samuel Smiles, one might say — and while he's prepared to be . . . philanthropic, sir, he also likes to see a commitment from the other side. But there's been some kind of palace revolution in the university — a disagreement about the funding, even with Mr Farmer supporting the project. So, he's not putting any more into it — for the time being, at least.'

Mrs Brent-Ellis snorted. 'So he's not just a soft touch, then.'

Karen Stannard nodded coolly. She did not care for Mrs Brent-Ellis but had her measure. 'I think that's an accurate summary.'

Mrs Brent-Ellis felt patronized, and she scowled. Her husband leaned forward hastily. He was well attuned to his wife's moods. 'This doesn't mean to say that the future of the project looks completely dark.'

Councillor Tremain's explosive grunt was contemptuous. 'It does at this end of the table. Let's be clear about this. If the purpose of this meeting is to try to get funding from the authority, that's a horse that won't run. We're already capped, overcommitted, with available funds completely allocated. There's no way we can raise money for anything new. If the project can't be covered by Brent-Ellis's own departmental funds the proposal is a waste of time.' He sniffed suspiciously. 'And if it *can* be so funded, that would imply you've already salted away some cash . . .'

'I assure you that isn't the case, Councillor,' Simon Brent-Ellis said hastily, and tugged at his moustache in a nervous gesture. 'We're fully committed and spent up, in terms of allocations—'

'But what's so important about this site, anyway?' his wife demanded, cutting across his discomfiture.

Karen Stannard glanced around. Her eyes lingered on Arnold for a moment, one eyebrow raised challengingly, as though she expected him to enter into dispute with her. Then her glance flickered away. 'I would consider that the Stangrove site is one of the most important areas for investigation within our county boundaries. It was originally thought that the enclosures were agricultural or settlement enclosures, but Mr Pym now believes they were more likely to have been sacred areas—'

'A temple or a church, you mean?' Selkirk asked.

'No, because the site is a very old one. We're talking perhaps of three thousand years. By a sacred site, I mean that it's highly likely the area was used for burial purposes. Mr Pym has already opened up one pit in which timber chambers had once been constructed. Unfortunately, it contained few grave goods and only some ceremonial urns. In other words, the burials there were cremations.'

Tom Patrick leaned forward; his handsome features marked with a frown. 'So if there's little to be found, why do you seek to plough more money into it? If the university isn't convinced—'

'Mr Pym is in dispute with others at the university. He feels there is a strong possibility that the other enclosures may contain burials that may have been more lavish — the chambered burial was a subsidiary one. That's his theory.'

'We can't put money into theories, or support the loser in an academic battle,' Tremain snapped disdainfully. 'I think this meeting is a waste of time, Chairman. There's no money, the project sounds to me a doubtful one, so what are we doing wasting time talking about it?'

Simon Brent-Ellis swallowed hard. It was rarely that he displayed the courage to argue with his paymasters, the elected members. 'I think, Councillor, Miss Stannard has found a way around the problem . . .'

Arnold caught the way in which Mrs Brent-Ellis glared at her husband. There was a steely glint in her eye which suggested to Arnold the lady was displeased that Brent-Ellis was supporting his deputy and all would not be harmony at the Brent-Ellis home that evening. She dragged her glance away from him towards Karen Stannard with reluctance, and only when she was satisfied her husband was aware of her displeasure.

'I repeat, Mr Pym feels the project is of major importance,' Karen Stannard was saying. 'And I concur with him, speaking as a professional. But of course, money is the issue. However, I've had the opportunity to speak at length with the site owner, Mr Farmer. There is a way in which he can be persuaded to lend some financial support.'

'Enough to pay for all of it?' Tremain sneered. 'I doubt that if he won't fund the university project.'

Karen Stannard shook her head. 'No, but he is prepared to make a *matching* contribution.'

Tremain's laugh was almost like a bark. 'Matching what? We've no cash to put in—'

'But the Lottery has,' Karen Stannard said quietly.

'The Lottery?' Tom Patrick stared at her in surprise. 'You're suggesting—'

'I've talked it over with Mr Farmer,' Karen Stannard said firmly. 'If we were able to obtain some Lottery funding and why shouldn't we? — he feels he would be able to bring together enough support in the business community to match the grant pound for pound. That is, of course, one of the prerequisites — to obtain Lottery funding we would have to demonstrate that we can obtain matching funding. Mr Farmer is agreeable.'

'Mr Farmer will have put a ceiling on it—'

'But of course.' She smiled. 'But it's quite a high ceiling. We could approach the Lottery committee for half a million.'

She paused and let the silence develop. 'If we do, he's confident he'll be able to match it through local contributions.'

There was a long silence in the room. Arnold caught the triumph in Karen Stannard's eyes as she sat there, watching the stunned faces. She was enjoying this moment. At last, Tom Patrick stirred in his chair. Thoughtfully, he smoothed the grey streaks above his right ear. He looked at her quizzically. 'A half-million . . . Farmer will put that much in?'

'If the Lottery bid is successful, he and others will contribute. And I've already made some soundings, Chairman. I've spoken to members of the Lottery committee and also to other people who have already made successful bids in other parts of the country. Using that information I've taken the trouble to sketch out the kind of submission we should be making—'

'You've been busy, Miss Stannard,' Councillor Tremain muttered uneasily. 'On what authority—'

'I had no *authority*, Councillor Tremain,' she flashed at him. 'I merely took it upon myself to investigate possibilities before it came to this sub-committee. I consider it's better to come forward with a worked-out proposal rather than talk airily about vague possibilities . . .'

'Even so . . .' Tremain grumbled. Arnold gained the impression he had come into the room desirous of scuppering the whole project and felt that he had been outmanoeuvred.

Councillor Selkirk, on the other hand, seemed to enjoy his colleague's discomfiture. 'I think it's a splendid idea, and I feel Miss Stannard is to be congratulated on her initiative. It seems to me, Chairman, that the council loses nothing by this — if the site is important, we can oversee its development. The Lottery money will come to us, I presume?'

Karen Stannard inclined her head gravely. 'A committee would need to be formed, to receive the grant.'

Selkirk beamed. 'So we needn't grub around in Tremain's financial pockets, we'll get support from this man Farmer and other businessmen, and we'll get a lot of good publicity. I move that we support Miss Stannard in this—'

'It was a departmental matter,' Mrs Brent-Ellis warned, while her husband shuffled uncomfortably.

'Of course, of course,' Selkirk replied hastily, having occasionally suffered the whiplash of his fellow councillor's tongue in formal meetings. 'Mr Brent-Ellis will clearly be in charge of this development, but since Miss Stannard has been the prime mover and shaker, I would suggest she be asked to carry on the good work — under Mr Brent-Ellis's supervision, of course —and complete the submission for the Lottery grant—'

'One moment.' Tom Patrick's head was lowered as he stared thoughtfully at his hands. 'I'm not sure that's the right way forward. We have to consider the manpower requirements in all this. Mr Brent-Ellis?'

'Sir?'

'How . . . *stretched* is your department?'

'Stretched?' Simon Brent-Ellis squinted at the ceiling, a little panicked. Arnold could see that he was frantically weighing his reply. An admission of the wrong kind could affect his golf afternoons. 'Well, I am forced to admit—'

'Could you afford, for instance, to release Miss Stannard from other activities so she could concentrate on this?'

The panic was now apparent in Brent-Ellis's features. 'Oh, I see, well, no, I have to say—'

'Or perhaps you yourself . . .' Patrick pressed.

'Me? Oh, no, sir. I couldn't possibly undertake a . . . major commitment to this project. There's the running of the department, and then of course, as you may have heard, I am also committed heavily to the conference that the department is co-hosting in a few weeks. It's a national conference, under the auspices of the Society of Professional Archaeologists . . .'

The SPA conference was one on which Brent-Ellis had in fact been spending very little time, having delegated most of the work to Arnold. He would be taking maximum advantage of it, of course, as he had already done with the planning sessions held at an hotel on the Northumberland coast, near Amble, but the greater part of the work was being done by Arnold. Brent-Ellis now glanced his way, uncertainly. 'Of course, we might be able to spare Mr Landon to do some support work on the submission—'

'No, that won't be possible,' Karen Stannard interrupted crisply. 'Mr Landon already has his hands full. He has a complete schedule of planning meetings, is working on several site developments, and is also the senior staff member in support of the director on the archaeological conference, which, I agree with Mr Brent-Ellis, is a prestigious affair. And I also agree that perhaps my time is limited, but even so I would be happy to burn the midnight oil on such a submission and I can assure the committee—'

She *wants* this, Arnold thought to himself. It was clear that Tom Patrick was also aware of her desires. He fixed her with a long, calculating glance. He raised a hand, silencing her, and nodded slowly. 'There's much to be said for your continued involvement with the submission, Miss Stannard — when you've put so much work into it. You've . . . ah . . . never before made an approach to the Lottery for funds?'

'No, sir, I—'

'And this is, as you say, an important project.' Tom Patrick leaned back in his chair and pulled at his lower lip thoughtfully. 'You're the deputy head of the department; Mr Brent-Ellis is already heavily involved in setting up a conference, in addition to his other duties; Mr Landon is not available, as you say. And you have no experience of such submissions.' When he looked up his grey eyes were expressionless. 'And it seems to me we need expert assistance on this whole thing.'

Karen Stannard's tone was cool. 'Chairman, I feel sure I can draw up an appropriate submission.'

'I'm sure you do *feel* that. Your confidence is praiseworthy. But I repeat, if this is so important, and it clearly is, we would be wise to seek an *experienced* hand at the wheel.'

Karen Stannard's eyes had darkened. She sat rigidly under the implied criticism, her back straight, her head up. She said nothing as she stared at Patrick. He was unabashed by her glare. He turned to his fellow councillors.

'I think that Miss Stannard has put forward an interesting and exciting possibility. She's to be commended for that. But a successful submission for Lottery funding . . . I think we need to undertake a trawl, find out who we might be able to appoint to write the submission and present it—'

'That will cost money, Chairman,' Karen Stannard objected.

'Isn't your time also money, Miss Stannard?' Mrs Brent-Ellis snapped, happy to get in a needle prick. She glared again at her husband triumphantly. Arnold gained the impression there was trouble of some kind between the two, and this meeting was helping exacerbate it.

Tom Patrick nodded, agreeing with his fellow councillor. 'That's right. There are staff costs if you draw up the submission, Miss Stannard — they can't be hidden. And you're all so *busy* . . .' He shook his head. 'No, if we are to be successful we need an expert, an outsider, someone who has experience of such submissions. I propose that we put out feelers, find who's available, and draw up a shortlist of people who might be able to help us.'

'But—'

Karen Stannard stopped speaking as Patrick glared at her coldly. 'Not that Miss Stannard's continued advice and support won't be welcome, of course,' he said. 'She's made the initial contact with our wealthy philanthropist. I think it would be most useful if she were to continue to *liaise* with him. And once we've made an appointment, the person we choose will be able to work closely with department personnel.' He smiled a tight smile in Karen Stannard's direction. 'There's nothing to stop you *seeking* the appointment, of course, Miss Stannard, and attending the interviews . . . though if we appointed you, it *would* mean you would have to relinquish your position in the department, naturally . . .'

When the meeting ended, the decision had been made.

* * *

'*Bastard*!'

Seated behind her desk, she almost spat out the word. Standing in front of her, Arnold waited. He had seen her angry before, but this mingling of anger and frustration was as bad as any he'd witnessed during the time they had worked together. She had instructed him to join her in her office, and he had no doubt its main purpose was to have someone on whom she could vent her anger. And anger did not detract from her beauty. Her eyes flashed, there was a heightened colour to her cheeks, and she looked magnificent.

'And you were no damned help, either!'

'How do you mean?' Arnold asked helplessly.

'You didn't say a bloody word!'

'What was I supposed to say? I've not been involved in the Stangrove Project. I know nothing about it. I've never even visited the site. You've been the only departmental person allowed near the place.'

'Are you criticizing me and the way I run this department?'

He was tempted to remind her it was Brent-Ellis's department and not hers, but that would inflame her even more. Instead, he said, 'I'm merely telling you the way it's been. How can I speak of Stangrove when I know nothing about it?'

'You should have supported me! Instead of sitting there with your mouth shut, while Brent-Ellis boasted about his piddling conference! And why it takes two of you, as well as me, to set that damned thing up, I'll never know.'

But she really knew the answer to that one. Brent-Ellis might wish it to be seen as his conference, so he could reap the kudos, but he was afraid to do anything without having his deputy at his side, and it was on Arnold that the work would really fall. He remained silent now, as Karen Stannard gradually regained control, blunted the edge of her temper. She shrugged, at last. 'So what do you think they'll do now?'

Arnold shook his head. 'Advertise. Take soundings. Hold interviews. Maybe find a crony—'

'They'll never give the task to one of their own!' She gave an exasperated snort. 'Even *they* are not that stupid. Not when there's so much money at stake. Well, to hell with them. This was all my idea. I thought about it. I've set all this up — including Alan Farmer's offer of support — and this is the thanks I get. Well, they can make fools of themselves. I wash my hands of it. They can just get on with it. I've got plenty enough to do as it is.' She glared at an immaculately manicured fingernail. 'Bastard!' she repeated.

Arnold waited. After a while, as she still stared gloomily at her fingernails, he asked, 'Is there anything else you need me for?'

'I don't *need* you, Landon, for anything,' she sneered. 'But now that my services have been so cavalierly dispensed with, I see no reason why I should spend any more time on the Stangrove Project. Which means you might as well take it over.' She opened the desk drawer in front of her and extracted a file. 'I will remain in nominal charge, of course, and if anything of importance arises that I need to know about I know I can count on you to report to me. *Can't I?*' she demanded.

'As always, Miss Stannard.'

She thought him insolent and glared at him, but said no more. She half threw the file across her desk. 'You can look through this, and then get up there at your convenience.'

Arnold nodded, took the file and returned to his own room. He glanced through the file briefly, and then set it on one side. He had other matters that were demanding his urgent attention, so he would not be able to turn to the Stangrove Project for several days. But as he worked on the papers on his desk, his mind strayed back to the sub-committee meeting, and the way Mrs Brent-Ellis had been glaring at her husband. All was not well between them, and he could not help wondering whether the flashpoint was Karen Stannard.

Mrs Brent-Ellis had probably heard the gossip that Karen Stannard was interested in power rather than men — but maybe she thought that in her husband the two were commingled. Arnold smiled at the thought, power and Brent-Ellis were mutually exclusive ideas. Simon Brent-Ellis was an incompetent, lazy buffoon and it was rumoured he owed his advancement to his wife's influence.

If so, Arnold thought to himself, it was now something that she possibly had come to regret.

Ten days had passed before Arnold found time in his busy schedule to drive north to the coast and take his first look at the Stangrove dig. He enjoyed the drive, because it was a warm and sunny Friday morning and he caught occasional glimpses of the sea, a deep blue stretching to a distant horizon, while inland rose the green-brown slopes of the Cheviot Hills, hazed with wispy clouds. Even so, he found his mind dwelling on the atmosphere in the office, for Karen Stannard's annoyance at the decision of the sub-committee to engage an outside consultant had not been alleviated. Councillor Tom Patrick's group had moved quickly. The rumours were that soundings had been made and a shortlist already drawn up of possible candidates for the consultancy. Karen Stannard regarded it as a slap in the face, a stealing of her own idea, and most staff in the department tried to avoid her and the blackness of her mood.

'They haven't even advertised the bloody job,' she growled at Arnold when he was called to her office to discuss the monitoring task at Stangrove. 'I can see what's going to happen — they'll hand the job on a plate to some incompetent friend of theirs, and it'll then be up to us to haul him out of the mire when he makes a complete hash of the whole damned thing. Or at least,' she glowered, 'it'll be up to *you* to do the hauling.'

She still seemed to blame him for a lack of support at the sub-committee meeting — but then, that was par for the course. Karen Stannard did not care to lose, and if she did, she tended to look for someone to blame. Arnold was usually the nearest to hand.

So getting away to the coast was a relief — it took a while before he could clear himself of the tensions of the office but by the time he began to run down towards the coastal road he was in a happier mood. It was a narrow road, running between high hedges that were bursting into leaf, and the overarching trees sent patterns of light and shade across his windscreen. He drove past an old railway cutting, and beyond that an iron bridge that would have been built in the Victorian period to give access to the gardens of a country manor, and then he was breasting a rise, swinging left along the coast road that led to Stangrove.

He could see a big house on his left, set back beyond a sturdy stone wall with a long gravelled drive leading up to it past a sentinel line of ancient beech trees. He drove on with the sound of the sea rumbling in through the open window, and in the distance he could see the dunes that had been raised by strong offshore winter winds. The road swung in a gentle curve along a lifting cliff line and he was looking down to an area of rock and sand and shingle. The cliff line would be ancient. Over the millennia the sea here would have retreated and the lower cliffs suffered from erosion until only the long, rocky, flat expanse he was looking down on had been left. From the geological maps he had found in Karen Stannard's file he had been able to see where the gravel pits had been dug, in front of the cliff line, and the archaeological site also had been delineated. It lay just a mile further on now, just below the crest of the cliff, protected from the sea winds, huddled under the shoulder of the hill.

He passed a farm then turned left. There was another ridge there, probably an even older line of cliff, and he turned into the wide stone track that had been cut out to provide egress for gravel lorries. The dust rose thickly as he bumped along over potholes and rough-hewn track.

There were several cars parked at the entrance to the quarry. He left his own car there and walked across to the huddle of buildings that had originally been used by the quarrymen as offices, but which clearly were now the centre of activity for the archaeological team. There was a man standing in the doorway of the nearest hut as Arnold walked forward. He was a big, shambling figure, carelessly dressed in a check open-necked shirt, worn jeans and toe-scuffed boots. He was smoking a pipe, leaning against the doorjamb and watching Arnold's approach with an air of quiet contemplation.

'Don't tell me,' he said as Arnold came up to him. 'You're from the county.'

'Is it that obvious?' Arnold said, smiling.

The big man shrugged and clamped his pipe stem in his back teeth. 'Not really. It's just that we've been expecting a visit after Karen Stannard rang a few days ago, and no one else much comes looking around here. The finds haven't been sensational enough to interest anyone else, so far.' He peered at Arnold inquisitively. 'Miss Stannard didn't sound too pleased when she rang.'

'She's been having problems,' Arnold replied shortly, extending his hand. 'My name's Arnold Landon.'

'George Pym. I'm in charge of the site. On sabbatical from York University. Come on inside — we're just taking a coffee break and looking over our working drawings.'

His back was broad, straining under the check shirt. He looked more like a logger than an academic, with his muscled arms and thick neck. He was about forty, Arnold guessed, a big man with thick black hair in which no hint of grey showed. His features were craggy, his skin tanned by wind and sun, and his hands were grubby. He shambled into the hut ahead of Arnold, calling out as he did so, 'Another mug of coffee, Sue — we got company.'

There were only the two of them in the hut. Arnold was introduced to Sue Lawrence, a colleague of Pym's from the university. She was a tall, rangy woman in her early thirties, whose fair hair was stuffed under a woolly cap. She wore a shapeless sweater and stained jeans, but her eyes were intelligent, her mouth generous, if somewhat discontented, and her handshake firm. He gained the impression she could be a formidable woman who cared little for her appearance when on site, but when Arnold saw the way George Pym looked at her he guessed also that the site director certainly was aware of her attractions.

'So,' Sue Lawrence began, cradling a coffee mug in her hands and looking directly into Arnold's eyes, 'what exactly is your place in the scheme of things?'

Arnold smiled. 'A small cog, believe me. Miss Stannard's been overlooking the work here as an observer, I understand — I suppose I'm just taking over from her. My function is to monitor what's going on, help in any way I can, and act as a link between what's happening and what's going to happen.'

Her eyes were sharp. 'By that, I suppose you mean this idea of a Lottery submission.'

Arnold shrugged. 'That's led to my involvement . . . But the submission itself is out of our hands, really. A consultant is being brought in—'

'So I gather. Anyone we know?'

'Not decided yet. They have a shortlist, I believe — and there'll be a committee to handle it. Miss Stannard will serve on that.'

'While you keep an eye on us.' There was no edge to her tone, and she watched him for a little while, sipping her coffee. 'I've heard of you.'

'Good or bad?' Arnold asked.

'Depends who you talk to.'

Such as Karen Stannard, Arnold thought. His relationship with her was an odd one. She was a woman who jealously guarded what she saw as her area of influence. She carried certain resentments, but there had also been times when he had caught her looking at him with an air of indecision, puzzlement . . . and there had been times when he felt she had been overtaken by a surge, an inclination . . . . Sue Lawrence was staring at him, with an odd half-smile on her lips. Arnold broke out of his reverie and turned to George Pym. 'I've seen the file Miss Stannard held, but you said you've been looking over some working drawings?'

'That's right,' Pym replied. 'We've got a small team down at the quarry itself, and I'll take you down there in a little while — in fact, it'll give you a chance to meet the land-owner, Alan Farmer, as well. He's down there this morning, watching the lads at it . . .' He frowned. 'They're not the best bunch, but all we can afford at the moment. They're from the Eastwood Training Agency . . . though what they're training for with us, God only knows! The agency is owned by one of your councillors — Tom Patrick.'

'I've met him.'

'It's a big business . . . We have them three weeks and they're gone again. Still . . . Working drawings. Come over here to the table, and you can see what we've been up to.'

The long deal table was covered with a series of drawings. Pym leaned over, pointing out the extent of the site and tracing the line of the old cliff edge, the slope that ran down to the quarry, the extent of the old gravel workings that Alan Farmer had discontinued when he purchased the land, and the archaeological dig area they were now working on.

'You'll see where the quarrying was in danger of destroying the likeliest area of the dig. If Alan Farmer hadn't come along it might have been lost forever. You see the ditches and the enclosure walls here? I've also got some old aerial photographs . . . see here. We estimate that the ditches and enclosures must have been dug some three thousand years ago, to enclose a sacrificial or burial site, and as soon as we started some serious work we found supportive evidence. A burial chamber, and dark earth deposits, which would suggest it was a plank-lined tomb . . .'

Arnold listened with interest as George Pym warmed to his explanation. He traced with his index finger the line of the old cliff, showed where the retreating sea must have formed a series of lagoons a thousand years ago, identified areas of lagoonal sediments in which they had found a series of short-lived butchery and knapping sites, and where they had found a tight cluster of flint flakes in a V-shaped pattern.

'So the whole area was an important hominid site, then?' Arnold asked.

'We think so.' George Pym nodded enthusiastically. 'Men and women would have lived and worked here for thousands of years, while their environment changed. The most dramatic discovery outside the enclosures is the horse butchery site in the lagoonal mud down here . . . It looks as though a group of hunters had killed a horse and butchered it. Half the bones have survived in the mud deposits — fragmentary and broken but we can work out from the marks on the bones how the animal was skinned, de-fleshed, disarticulated — a colleague of ours, Paul Samuels, has been doing that work. He's down at the site at the moment. He's even shown us how the bones were fractured to remove the marrow. And how, once the hunters moved on, the scavengers moved in — the bones were gnawed by carnivores, the gnaw marks overlaying the cut marks.' He grinned. 'The humans removed all the best bits first.'

'And there are knapping areas around the butchery site,' Sue Lawrence added, 'where they worked on flints even while they were cutting up the carcase.'

'It's like a snapshot in time — a few days, maybe, in eons, millennia.' George Pym shook his head. 'I still feel the thrill of it, after all these years. People working here and leaving their traces . . . *living* people.'

'While in the enclosures, a short distance away . . .' Arnold murmured.

'The rites of death.'

Pym took Arnold to the far end of the hut and pointed out the anvils they had discovered — large unmodified lumps of flint with one battered side — and hammer stones made of pebbles. He emphasized that the episode described by the remains must have occurred when the foreshore was covered with lagoons long since disappeared. But it was dramatic evidence of human activity. 'But that's all we could afford to do with the university team,' he added. 'Our funding was restricted. We couldn't raise a full team, just Paul Samuels and ourselves, so we concentrated on the lagoonal deposits. Until Mr Farmer entered discussions with Karen Stannard about the further investigation of the quarry site.'

'I'm still not clear about the relationship between the quarry site and your foreshore discoveries,' Arnold said.

Sue Lawrence moved away from the table. 'Maybe we'd better show Mr Landon the main site, George. So he can see how important it is.'

They walked slowly away from the huts towards the quarry, and Sue Lawrence explained to Arnold that her particular line of study was small mammal skeletons, of which she was making a study for a book. She launched into an earnest monologue on the teeth of water voles. It seemed that primitive voles had rooted teeth, whereas just before the Anglian Glaciation — almost five hundred thousand years ago — voles had developed continuously growing teeth.

'And that's a refinement we humans haven't yet aspired to!' she exclaimed triumphantly, her eyes shining. Arnold caught the indulgent smile that George Pym gave her, and was amused.

The quarry site was larger than Arnold had anticipated. He'd noted the raised enclosures and the surrounding ditches that had been delineated in the file drawings and realized they had crossed them in their walk, but the quarry itself was entered by way of a fairly steep decline beyond which the old gravel pits could be seen. But the excavations were being undertaken on a flat area that at the far end sloped up to the rise of the cliffs. A small hut guarded the area, and there were four young people scratching away in a desultory manner in sections marked out carefully by coloured streamers and ropes. There were two men standing there watching them, the shorter talking earnestly to his companion. George Pym made his way directly across to them.

'Mr Landon, shall I introduce you? This is Paul Samuels.' Samuels was short, slim, with belligerent eyes and an aggressive mouth. His hair was cropped close to his skull and he was unshaven, dark stubble marking his jawline. His handshake was competitive and he seemed slightly annoyed that he had been interrupted in his discussion with the other man.

'And this is Alan Farmer, the owner of the site on which we're working — and our benefactor, of course!'

Farmer was dressed in a Norfolk jacket which he filled comfortably. He was about forty-five — younger than Arnold had anticipated — and of military bearing, very upright, very confident. At some stage his nose had been broken and badly set, and it gave his face a slightly lopsided look. His eyes were somewhat narrowly set, pale blue and perceptive. He was taller than Arnold, something above six feet, and his voice was modulated, betraying a hint of a West Country accent. 'You've come to look over the site?'

'And see how I can help.'

'You work with Karen Stannard. An . . . interesting woman.'

It was an easy comment to agree with. Farmer glanced at his watch, as Paul Samuels muttered something about getting back to work and sidled away reluctantly. Farmer nodded. 'Yes, I must get back to the house, also. I've got a number of calls to make. It's strange, even though one retires, there are still demands on one's time.' He hesitated, glancing uncertainly at Arnold. 'I'm sorry to rush away like this, but I take it you'll be here all day?'

'That's right,' Arnold replied. 'And then I make my way across towards Amble. There's a planning meeting there for the archaeological conference—'

'Hah! I see. Well, as I say, I must rush back, but in the circumstances, why don't you come down to lunch at the manor house this afternoon.' Farmer flicked a glance at

George Pym and Sue Lawrence. 'That includes any of you who can get away, of course. Give us a chance to talk further about the site's future.' He hesitated, watching from the corner of his eye as Paul Samuels rejoined the young workers. 'Rather than discuss television matters . . .'

Arnold accepted the invitation, as did Sue Lawrence, but George Pym suggested he should stay on site with Samuels to keep an eye on the young men assisting them. As Alan Farmer walked away towards the Land Rover he had parked at the far end of the quarry, Pym clucked his tongue. 'He seems glad to get away. Paul must have taken the chance to corner him again. Alan Farmer has television interests, did you know? And Paul . . . well, he's been involved in a bit of a shouting match recently. I don't think he stands much of a chance. Approaching Farmer isn't going to do his cause much good, but then, we know Paul, don't we . . . ?'

Sue Lawrence murmured assent, and then turned away. 'If we're to go to lunch, Mr Landon needs a quick tour . . .'

They spent the next two hours walking around the site.

It was clear that the quarry had broken into what had once been a fairly large burial area, if the ditches and enclosures were anything to go by. There were in fact four enclosures, only one of which had been opened up to date. The first was where they had discovered the planked chamber and the cremation urn.

'Unfortunately,' George Pym explained, 'following the cremation, the grave goods were broken and only a few fragments found their way into the backfilling of the chambers. But we have higher hopes of the others. The chances are they might be of later date . . . and from their size, I suspect they'll be of more importance.'

Arnold was inclined to agree. The three further enclosed areas, complete with bank and ditch, were laid out on the gentle slope that led to the ancient cliff tops, now seen only as a ridge overlooking the former foreshore. Two of them had been stripped of topsoil, but little more had been done. Shortage of labour, Pym explained. But he gave an interesting scenario, covering what he expected to find in such a site. From the finds at the ancient lagoons below it would appear that hominid activity would have been widespread in the area, but the relative position and lack of signs of agricultural or settlement activity on the ridge would suggest that the quarry area would have had considerable religious significance. Pym was certain it was a burial ground, and one that could be rich in archaeological interest.

It was a theme Sue Lawrence expounded on further when she and Arnold had lunch at Stangrove Hall with Alan Farmer. It was a light lunch, eaten in the relative simplicity of the small dining room just adjacent to Farmer's study. They took a glass of red wine with him, and Sue Lawrence talked.

'You need to see it as a line of cliffs that at one time must have run for twenty miles north of here. The cliffs still survive, but not much more than six metres in height, and almost totally masked by erosion. Originally, of course, they would have been as tall as Beachy Head, maybe, but there was a time when the sea levels were so much higher and a storm bank beached up against the cliffs. I think some of the earliest remains we've found must have been rolled out into the beach gravels at the foot of the cliffs.'

'I suppose the beach would have been a popular place for early man, because of the availability of flint,' Arnold suggested.

'That's right. It would be revealed in the constant cliff falls. Then, as the sea levels fell a series of lagoons built up, the sea retreated further, the lagoons dried up and the earthworms moved in and formed soil. Plants grew, and there would have been a grassy plain, scrub, bushes, deer, horses, bison, rhinos . . . even elephants, possibly . . . and that's the area where we've found the knapping site, and the butchery activity . . .'

It was always interesting to listen to an enthusiast. Arnold watched her as she talked, noted her animation and how, as she became more excited, her eyes flashed and her colour rose. He had detected a warmth in the manner in which George

Pym had looked at her, and he could appreciate the man's interest. If Sue Lawrence took more care with her appearance she could be a very attractive woman. Though that was hardly a fair comment, he thought to himself, since she was dressed for grubbing around in the soils of the quarry site.

'Are you going to be involved in this archaeological conference, Miss Lawrence?' Alan Farmer asked, over coffee.

She shook her head. 'No, my own specialism is small mammals, and they've got a big shot from London to talk about that. I might attend some of the sessions, if I think them worthwhile.'

'There's to be a cocktail reception at the commencement of the conference,' Farmer said.

'I don't imagine I'll be invited.'

He smiled. 'I'm sure you will, if I use my influence.' He glanced at Arnold, noting the way he was taking in his surroundings. 'Mr Landon, would you care to look around the house?'

Sue Lawrence hastily excused herself, as Arnold said he would indeed like to be taken around Stangrove Hall. She had work to do back at the quarry but was quite happy to walk back. After seeing her to the drive, Alan Farmer returned and then gave Arnold a conducted tour, explaining that the older part of the house was Elizabethan. After a while, as they progressed from room to room, Farmer began to ask questions rather than give information as he realized the extent of Arnold's knowledge of mediaeval houses. Arnold was able to satisfy the owner's curiosity about what would have been the great hall, and the guest lodgings that would have been provided in the extending lateral wings built later in the period. The house was an interesting one: two show fronts with one containing the remains of a gatehouse, garret bedrooms — probably for children rather than servants — and lateral gables, rather than the dormers that were more commonly favoured in Europe at that time.

'The complete mediaeval three-storeyed house,' Arnold enthused. 'There'd have been no provision for access between apartments but this would have been a long gallery — a sort of indoor promenade from which you could have gained access to the bedrooms. You can still see the remains of the construction, in the beams above . . . And the owners would probably have brought in craftsmen in wood, stone and plaster from the Continent, to achieve these effects . . .'

'I hadn't realized workers were so mobile in the period,' Farmer mused.

'They certainly were — masons and woodwrights were brought in from all over Europe, not just other parts of England. The fifteenth century produced magnificent timber manor houses and over the next two hundred years the western masons raised equally impressive houses of stone.'

'But it takes a manufacturer of computer software to be able to afford the maintenance of such structures today,' Farmer said almost ruefully.

'At least you've had the good sense to retire early, and enjoy such a magnificent building as this. Though as you said earlier, retirement doesn't mean that you vegetate, exactly.'

'That's true.' Farmer laughed shortly as they made their way back down the magnificent staircase. 'I sold my major shareholding in the software company I set up in Swindon, bought into a company producing programmes for television, just as a minor interest, really, and came here — but there always seems to be some little problem or other popping up. Paul Samuels was talking to me . . .' He paused. 'But then, I shouldn't bore you with his problems . . .' He stopped at the foot of the stairs and gazed around. 'But I'm happy here . . . even if it does get a bit lonely. My wife died, some four years ago.'

'I'm sorry to hear that.'

Farmer brushed the matter aside, as though slightly embarrassed that he had mentioned it. 'And you're going on now to this conference meeting up at Amble.'

Arnold smiled. 'It's hardly a hardship. It's being held in the country club there — somewhat lavish for holding planning meetings but since that's where the conference is to be held it was decided to have the planning meetings there also, as part of the package deal.' Privately, he thought it a waste of time and money, but if it meant a weekend in some luxury at the county's expense, he supposed he should hardly criticize the system.

'Miss Stannard is on the planning committee, I understand.'

'That's right.'

'I've been spending some time with her, while she's been visiting the Stangrove dig. It was she who came up with the idea of a Lottery grant, and persuaded me to match it. It seemed a sensible way to spend some money.' He smiled. 'And the site won't get developed without a considerable amount of financing.' He walked with Arnold towards the door. 'You . . . you'll know Miss Stannard quite well.'

'I've worked with her for a few years now,' Arnold replied, somewhat evasively.

'What's your opinion of her? I mean . . . what's she really like?'

Arnold was suddenly at a loss. The question was too open-ended, and he did not know Alan Farmer, or the reason for his interest. He shrugged. 'She's very able, intelligent and hard-working. She doesn't suffer fools gladly, but she doesn't ask you to do anything she feels she's not capable of doing herself.' And she can use her tongue like a knife or like a pick handle, he thought — arguments with her could be bruising. They were thoughts he did not express to Alan Farmer.

'She's a very beautiful woman,' Farmer said quietly. 'Does she . . . is she in any relationship, that you're aware of?'

Arnold expelled his breath doubtfully. 'I'm afraid I can't tell you, Mr Farmer. She'll have a life outside the office, of course, but I'm not a close friend of hers and I don't think I could say . . .'

'I was merely curious. She can be very . . . charming.' And deadly, Arnold thought to himself. If the question had been asked of others in the Morpeth office it was likely Alan Farmer would have been given rather more information concerning rumours, at least. Arnold didn't feel it was his part to pass on such rumours, or to suggest that if Farmer was interested in a personal relationship with Karen Stannard he might find he was doomed to disappointment. But then, after all, though Karen Stannard was an ambitious woman, with a clear view of her priorities in life, Alan Farmer was a rich man . . .

And Arnold Landon still found certain enigmatic qualities in Karen Stannard which made him realize that he still did not really know what made her tick . . .

3

This was the third occasion on which the SPA conference committee had met in the country club. A pattern had been developed: they arrived at the hotel early on the Friday evening, held a short meeting before dinner, and then had a full committee meeting on the Saturday, before dispersing to go their separate ways on Sunday morning. The Saturday evening dinner, after the main meeting, was designed as an opportunity to relax and should have been a pleasant enough occasion, with wine provided at the county's expense, while other expenses were covered by the conference budget itself, but it tended to be a somewhat jagged affair socially.

The SPA conference had been run successfully for some ten years under the chairmanship of Colin Norfolk and drew professional archaeologists from all over the country, with a few delegates from Europe and the occasional visitor from the States. It was the first time Arnold had been involved in its planning, and he felt that the county presence was somewhat overstated with himself, Brent-Ellis and Karen Stannard all in attendance, but the committee seemed to know what it was doing, with a history of successful ventures behind it.

Even so, he found the make-up of the committee some-what odd. To begin with it was too large to be completely efficient, comprising ten archaeologists — seven men and three women — who had decided views about their own specialist areas. And it included a husband-and-wife team: while Colin Norfolk was in the chair, his wife Sheila Norfolk was long established as conference secretary. They appeared to be barely speaking to each other. It tended to make the social intentions of the Saturday night dinner somewhat difficult to achieve.

During the committee sessions Sheila Norfolk busied herself with note-taking and made little contribution to the discussion. Outside the meetings when the pair were together there was an air of crackling tension between them. The main body of the committee barely seemed to notice. They were all too much involved in their own esoteric discussions, or perhaps they were well used to the situation. As for Simon Brent-Ellis, he was too self-centred, too concerned with making a good impression to notice anything untoward. But Karen Stannard was aware of it, Arnold was certain.

The Friday evening session was chaired efficiently by Colin Norfolk. He was a lean, elegant man who cared for clothes: well-cut jacket, flowered tie, expensive shirt. His hair was thick, swept back neatly and his handsome, narrow features, casual air and light touch in directing the committee were clearly appreciated by the two middle-aged, rather dowdy female archaeologists on the committee who obviously thought he was wonderful and gushingly told Sheila Norfolk how lucky she was, in the bar after the meeting was over. Sheila Norfolk was unappreciative of the comments.

She herself was restrained. In her mid-forties, she dressed smartly if simply, had a good figure and deep-set, rather shadowed eyes, and a somewhat surly mouth. She said little. Arnold had found himself at the corner of the hotel bar in her company for a short while, and he had thought her heavy going. She drank gin and tonic and did not stint herself, but she was moody, disinclined to small talk, and her eyes never seemed to be still. But her glance usually returned to her husband, chatting casually with one or the other of the females, and then her eyes were full of resentment.

She was also watchful during the whole of the Friday evening, as far as Karen Stannard was concerned.

The Saturday morning session of the committee was fruitful. The programme that was being planned for the conference was wide-ranging. It was to be held over three days, and individual presenters were encouraged to produce written papers, to which they would speak for a limited period only. Evening sessions at the conference were planned as interest groups, following up on topics that had been presented on the day.

'So we've got the skeleton in place, if you'll pardon the archaeological expression,' Colin Norfolk announced, as one of his female admirers giggled at the weak joke. 'We have on the first day a contribution on the analytical work being undertaken to define the presence of foodstuff residues in pottery vessels — we're calling that . . . ?'

'Leaf Wax in Antiquity,' Sheila Norfolk muttered, consulting her notes.

'Then we have the Swedish professor who'll be discussing the ethical principles involved in excavating human skeletal remains, followed by a session on ancient DNA, and one on Mesolithic lake sites.' He paused, gnawing elegantly on his lower lip. 'I think that is followed by—'

'Biomolecular Palaeontology,' Sheila Norfolk snapped impatiently, and Colin Norfolk grimaced. Arnold glanced at her. She was clearly on edge. She caught his glance, held it directly, one eyebrow raised as though challenging him. He looked away. This was no quarrel of his.

There was a long discussion thereafter about whether the session she had mentioned should take place on the first day or should be held over for the second. The committee was subjected to a pompous harangue from Bernard Hewlett, a professor from York University and an acknowledged expert on biomolecular evolution. He argued that the topic area should be extended into discussion groups on the second day as well as the first. 'We have several approaches worth discussion,' he boomed. 'Survey and evolution of proteins and lipids, decay and preservation of organic matter, inter-laboratory verification . . .'

'We simply don't have time,' Sheila Norfolk said irritably. 'The conference is planned to cover a wide range of topic areas—'

'Too wide, one would say,' Hewlett interrupted. He was a tall man in his late fifties, of serious countenance, grim-visaged, balding badly. He was a man used to getting his own way, and had a reputation for being short-tempered. He was irritated now. It was clear he did not care for Sheila Norfolk.

The feeling was clearly reciprocated. 'If every *expert* insisted on a larger share of the conference cake,' she sneered, 'we'd be running for a month, not three days. The programme has already been determined. The topics agreed. It's all a matter of balance. Something Mr Hewlett seems to lack.'

Hewlett's eyes bulged, and he was about to respond angrily when the chairman held up a hasty hand. 'I think it's time we adjourned for coffee. We can return to this later . . .'

Sheila Norfolk tapped her pencil impatiently on her notebook, and the committee broke up, heading into the small anteroom where coffee cups had been laid out for them, with a waiter hovering in attendance. Arnold noted that Colin Norfolk drew his wife aside and spoke to her in an urgent undertone. She glared at him sullenly for a while, and then turned away with an air of indifference before he had finished talking.

At Arnold's elbow, Karen Stannard murmured, 'Marital harmony disturbed, would you say, Landon?'

The topic raised by Hewlett was not referred to again when the committee reconvened — Colin Norfolk moved on swiftly to other matters, and Hewlett simmered in a sulky silence.

Arnold sat with Simon Brent-Ellis at lunch, while Karen Stannard joined Colin Norfolk. They seemed to be having an animated discussion over a bottle of wine. Sheila Norfolk sat apart, watching them with subdued fury in her eyes. Arnold felt a little sorry for her, she was clearly troubled.

The afternoon session continued with the planning, and gradually the form of the whole conference took shape. Arnold was impressed by the list of speakers the committee had managed to recruit. It included eminent names in the field. By five o'clock Colin Norfolk declared himself satisfied. There was little more that now needed to be done.

'I think we'll need no further full meetings of the committee' except for our usual meeting immediately before the conference itself,' he suggested. 'It only requires final checks on administrative arrangements and we've already agreed on a small sub-committee which Sheila will organize to tidy up the loose ends. Which means, first, that I can thank you for all the hard work you've put in over these last few months, and second, that I can now invite you all to have a drink with me in the bar before dinner.'

There was a murmur of pleased assent. Arnold had intended to take a swim in the hotel pool before dinner but felt it would be churlish to absent himself after Norfolk's invitation. So he went along with the others, and took a seat in the corner, listening vaguely to the conversation between two of the committee members about dating methods on animal bones, until one of the younger members, Gareth Robbins, hovered over him and asked him if he'd like a drink. Arnold accepted the offer and on his return from the bar Robbins slid into the seat beside him. 'So, Landon, we've not really had the chance for a chat so far. You work for the county, of course, I know that, but where did you train? Which university?'

Tall, skinny and sandy-haired, Robbins was reputed to be the youngest man holding a chair in archaeology, albeit at one of the newer universities, and there was a brashness about him that was almost refreshing in contrast to the staider members of the committee. His interventions in committee were usually cheerful, and apposite, and Arnold liked him. 'I didn't go to university.'

'Ahah! The School of Life, hey? Which probably means you know a damn sight more about digs than any of us here.

That's the problem with university training in our discipline — you tend to have a narrow, stereotyped view of life, and never get too far away from the lecture theatre and the research laboratory. Gives rise to a dislike of having your ideas queried — like Hewlett this morning, for instance.' He grinned disarmingly. 'Whereas you . . . you'll have grubbed it all out at the coal face, so to speak.'

Arnold laughed. 'I can't say I've heard my situation put so supportively before! Though perhaps a little inaccurately.'

Robbins sniffed. 'Ah, well, casting light in dark corners and all that. We academics need a kick up the practical backside from time to time. I've heard a lot about you, Landon — I understand you are reputed to have a flair.'

'Is that what it's called?'

'Not the kind of flair that our chairman has, of course,' Robbins muttered, glancing around as one of the women sitting with Colin Norfolk shrieked with laughter, with her hands to her face at his outrageousness. 'He's a respected writer on biblical archaeology, but religion doesn't seem to have rubbed off on him, other than in Old Testament horniness. His wife has had a rough time, I believe it's said he can't keep his hands off the female students. Or fellow archaeologists, it seems.' He glanced across the room to where Sheila Norfolk was sitting with Simon Brent-Ellis and Karen Stannard. 'Still, his missus looks a bit happier at the moment — now that your colleague isn't being ogled by her husband.'

He looked at Arnold, quizzically. 'How would you rate our chairman's chances with your colleague, Miss Stannard? Stunning looker. Saw her in close proximity chat with Norfolk earlier on at lunch. He seemed . . . enamoured. His wife thought so too. Maybe that's why she's staying close now — crowding out the opposition. Though I'm amazed that she still cares.'

Arnold shook his head. 'I'd be surprised if Mr Norfolk . . . well, let's just say I think Karen Stannard is rather selective in the company she keeps.'

'Which Norfolk isn't — that's a fact. He'll lay anything in a skirt, so they say. There was a blow-up recently, I believe, between the Norfolks. Maybe she's coming to the end of her tether. Wouldn't surprise me if she put a knife into him sometime. Or maybe removed the appendages that cause the trouble . . .'

They carried on a desultory conversation until it was time for dinner. The seating was flexibly arranged, but Arnold noted that Colin Norfolk had managed to obtain a seat beside Karen Stannard once again, and was engaging her in conversation, leaning in her direction, and gazing into her eyes. She seemed somewhat bored, and Arnold caught her glance several times. He suspected she was too aware of the tension between husband and wife to play up to the committee chairman. Not that she wouldn't have done so, if she'd had good reason, like a warning off from his wife, but possibly her bar conversation with Sheila Norfolk had led her to believe it was something she should not get involved in.

As for Sheila Norfolk herself, she had clung to Brent-Ellis as they made their way into dinner and she seemed to be in a happier, almost flirtatious mood. The drink in the bar and the wine on the table had probably enlivened her and allowed her to forget her anxieties. She was being very charming to Simon Brent-Ellis. He in his turn was demonstrating that though he might be lazy and incompetent in the office, he was certainly capable of being attentive to a reasonably attractive woman.

Most of the group returned to the bar after dinner and sat in small groups discussing their archaeological experiences. Arnold decided after taking coffee that it would be a good idea to take a walk, and then try a late-night swim — if the pool was still open.

The hotel was designated as a country club and it did possess a nine-hole golf course, wooded at the far end where it overlooked the sea. There was a half-moon and the sky was clear; Arnold strolled through the garden and along the track to the woods. An owl screeched in the darkness ahead of him. The air was cool and he was aware of the sea breeze rustling through the trees. He stood on the foreshore for a while, staring out to sea, with the lights of Amble across to his left. He found himself wondering what Jane Wilson was doing at the moment. She had taken a contract to write a book in the States, and somehow or other the period had been extended. She had given him no date for her return, and there were times when he really missed her. But, rather guiltily, he admitted to himself that in one way her absence made things easier, gave him time to try to evaluate their relationship. They had been friends for years, lovers more recently, but he suspected she wanted from him a commitment greater than he was able — or prepared — to give at this stage. It was a reluctance he could not explain to himself, let alone to her.

He wandered aimlessly on the foreshore for some time, his thoughts drifting between Jane, and the Stangrove Project, the finds that had been made in the ancient lagoons and the possibilities that lay at the dig itself. Finally, he made his way back to the hotel. He looked in at the bar, bought himself a nightcap but avoided the groups chatting together. Brent-Ellis, he noted, was sitting with Karen Stannard and Sheila Norfolk again, and appeared to be enjoying himself. Arnold made no attempt to join them, but went up to his room and read for a while.

He had missed the opportunity for a swim earlier. Finally, he went back downstairs. The receptionist was accommodating. The pool was normally closed after eight in the evening, but they were prepared to allow him to enter. He spent an hour in the pool, working off the effects of the dinner and the alcohol, and then, with a towel over his arm he made his way back along the corridor to the lifts.

He was vaguely aware of a woman standing at the house phone as he pressed for the lift, but barely glanced at her. He checked his watch; he was surprised at the lateness of the hour. There was a subdued murmur from the bar. It was just on midnight but there were still some people drinking there.

The lift was slow. He glanced up to the indicator: the lift seemed to be stuck at the fourth floor. And while he stared up he suddenly realized the identity of the woman at the house phone. It was Councillor Brent-Ellis, wife of the Director of the Department of Museums and Antiquities.

From where he stood at the lift, Arnold had sight of the reception area and as he waited he realized Mrs Brent-Ellis had failed to contact the person she was ringing. He saw her leaving the house phone, banging it down in irritation. She was clearly in a short-tempered mood. He caught a glimpse of her as she swept towards reception. There was a grim, determined expression on her stern features.

The receptionist was young, inexperienced and easily browbeaten.

'My husband is registered here,' Mrs Brent-Ellis snapped. 'Could I have a spare room key, please?'

'I'm sorry, madam, it's unusual if you yourself are not registered—'

'My husband is. I need to see him urgently. I've driven up from Morpeth. A key, please.'

Nervously, the girl checked the register and produced a spare key card. 'If you think it's all right . . . It's 307. You just have to insert it in the—'

'I'm fully aware of how key cards operate,' Mrs Brent-Ellis snapped. She turned, and marched away towards the lift.

It was just arriving. Arnold looked at her uncertainly.

She glared at him, knowing him well enough, but affecting not to recognize him. As the lift doors opened Arnold hesitated; Mrs Brent-Ellis swept past him and entered the lift, grim-visaged. He was suddenly reluctant to enter the lift with her and endure a painful silence, in company with a woman clearly enraged. He held back, muttering he had forgotten something, and the lift doors closed in his face, with Mrs Brent-Ellis still refusing to acknowledge that she knew him.

He stood there awkwardly, vaguely annoyed with himself for his weakness. But he did not care for Mrs Brent-Ellis, she was a shrewish woman who kept her husband on a tight rein. He watched as the indicator light flickered, she was getting out at Arnold's floor. He doubted this visit was connected with council business. He could guess what was on her mind.

It was well known in the department that she had long since regretted allowing the appointment of Karen Stannard to the post of deputy to her husband. She had heard the rumours of Karen Stannard's sexual predilections, of course, but Arnold suspected that she discounted them with disbelief. Eleanor Brent-Ellis was no fool. All that talk about Karen Stannard being uninterested in men, possibly a lesbian, she would know it for what it was — ill-informed gossip.

She was a possessive woman, and she had long been unhappy at the fact that her husband was now working with a young, beautiful, confident woman who turned heads everywhere she went. Rumour had it she seethed at meetings when Karen Stannard was present. Jerry Picton regularly regaled the department with anecdotes about the treatment she gave her husband if she even suspected him of spending time in his deputy's presence, outside meetings. She had made it known that she had little regard for Karen Stannard's talents or professionalism, but there she was acknowledged to be on weak ground.

The lift was on the way back down.

Arnold sighed. He could guess that these weekends would have caused a problem in the Brent-Ellis household. It was said that Mrs Brent-Ellis was a believer in substitution theory: if her husband spent his time playing golf his mind would not turn to sex. Jerry Picton reckoned she was not interested in either activity, but wanted her husband firmly exhausted by long drives rather than furtive couplings. Arnold could not imagine where Picton received his information. But that she was a jealous woman was quite clear to everyone.

And these weekends . . . inevitably they would not please her. When it was first mooted that the county should support and help organize the SPA conference, Brent-Ellis had eulogized it as a feather in the cap of his department, the mounting of a prestigious national conference that would bring together notable people from all over the country. She had publicly thrown cold water on it all, but had not prevailed in council.

Arnold entered the lift and pressed the button for his floor. He smiled ruefully, guessing at the conversation that would now be going on in Brent-Ellis's room. She would be in there, breathing fire, complaining that she saw no need for him to serve on the committee, spending weekends away from home in a luxurious hotel. And Karen Stannard's presence on the same committee, and in the same hotel would be adding fuel to an already blazing fire of resentment.

Arnold was convinced that there was no cause for Mrs Brent-Ellis's jealousy of Karen Stannard. He knew that she held her director in little regard and suffered his weak leadership with scant respect. Whether the rumours that she was not interested in men were right or wrong, Arnold suspected that Simon Brent-Ellis would be the last person that Karen Stannard would turn to in personal terms, however professionally ambitious she might be.

When Arnold stepped out of the lift on the third floor he was immediately embarrassed. He had thought to avoid Mrs Brent-Ellis but he now caught sight of her at the end of the corridor, a thickset, middle-aged woman in high dudgeon, and set on a confrontation. She was standing outside her husband's bedroom door, leaning forward, listening, and as Arnold began to walk towards her she inserted the key card and opened the door, rushing inwards with a snort of anger.

There was a short silence, and then the bedroom lights flashed on and all hell seemed to break loose. Arnold was drawing level with the doorway when the screaming began. As he passed and glanced into the room he saw Mrs Brent-Ellis's broad back, arms raised in fury, and realized it was her voice he had heard, hysterical with rage. He stopped, uncertain what to do. Beyond the furious woman he caught a glimpse of a heaving, wriggling couple in the bed, Simon Brent-Ellis's face staring wildly at his wife, open-mouthed with astonishment over a woman's naked shoulder and then there was a riot of bedclothes as the coverlet was thrown back, the woman was almost jerked aside to tumble sideways to the carpeted floor, and Simon Brent-Ellis rolled out of bed, white-faced, grabbing for his groin as though to deny his wife sight of the evidence of his passion. Arnold caught a brief flash of his plump, middle-aged bottom and then he decided he had better walk away from the domestic scene — none of his business — as the wronged wife roared her anger and her pain and her fury. 'I'll have your *guts* for this, Simon Brent-Ellis!'

But as Arnold walked away quickly towards his own room he was astonished to hear, 'And as for you, I'll have you drummed out of the department, you two-faced, sluttish whore! Stannard, I'll make sure you won't get another job in—'

Incredulous, Arnold stopped in his tracks. He glanced back down the corridor, towards the open bedroom door. Karen Stannard? In bed with Brent-Ellis? He was astounded, unable to believe it. Then he heard the tone change in Mrs Brent-Ellis's voice. '*Who the hell are you?*'

Confused, Arnold stood in the corridor, consumed with curiosity of the kind he deprecated in Jerry Picton, and yet unable to move as the scene was played out in Brent-Ellis's bedroom. There was a short silence, the sound of another woman's voice, and then Mrs Brent-Ellis's fury roared back. 'You swine!' she raged, and there was the crashing sound of a chair being overturned. 'You've got *two* of them in tow! After all the years I've devoted to you, to your career, to your advancement, to your home comforts — this is the way you treat me! I'll see to it, Brent-Ellis, that you'll—'

'Please . . . Eleanor, please.' There was another crash, a gagging sound and a brief silence. Arnold hesitated, uncertain what to do, and turned to head for his own room. Then at once both women in the room began screaming. This time it was not fury. Arnold detected the sound of sheer panic.

It spurred him from his indecision. He turned back, ran towards Brent-Ellis's room.

In the doorway he could see Simon Brent-Ellis was out of bed, gagging, staring up at his vengeful wife. But it was not the pleading look that forcefully struck Arnold: it was the colour of Brent-Ellis's face. The man was on his knees, naked, still clutching an ineffectual hand at his genitals, but his face was white, his mouth open and drooling and he pawed the air with his left hand as though trying to brush away cobwebs. 'Eleanor,' he gasped, and then as both women screamed again he pitched forward on his face, hitting the floor with a thud to groan once, and lie there motionless.

Eleanor Brent-Ellis stared down at her prostrate husband. 'Get up and stop playing the fool! You don't get away with that weak-kneed nonsense!'

He made no response.

She turned, to glare again at the woman standing at the other side of the bed. 'This is all *your* doing!' she snarled.

Shocked, the woman stared back at her, one hand clutching a blouse to her naked breast. 'Is he . . . is he dead?'

'*Dead*?' Strangely enough, Eleanor Brent-Ellis had clearly failed to consider the possibility. She thought that, coward as he was, he was feigning unconsciousness. 'Simon?' she queried sharply, turning to prod him with her foot. Then, when the man on the floor did not move, she said again, more demandingly, '*Simon!*'

Brent-Ellis remained motionless. Eleanor Brent-Ellis suddenly became aware of Arnold, standing in the doorway. She stared at him, open-mouthed and then as he hurried forward, concerned about Brent-Ellis, she let out a piercing cry. Arnold knelt beside the prostrate man, turning him over. There was a hissing sound coming from the man's mouth, a line of white spittle on his lips. Arnold reached for the phone, dialled for reception. He stared at Mrs Brent-Ellis, and at the other — naked — woman in the room. It was not Karen Stannard.

'Hello? Room 307. An ambulance — quickly!'

Suddenly, the room was very silent.

CHAPTER TWO

1

'It's a bad business, a very bad business.'

The sunshine glinted through the office windows on Chief Executive Powell Frinton's glasses. It had the odd effect of rendering his eyes invisible to Arnold, not that there was much to be read in Powell Frinton's eyes at the best of times. He was a lean, ascetic-featured lawyer and a cold man, reserved, not given to expressing opinions unless they were professionally called for. He clearly considered the present situation highly embarrassing.

'How is Mrs Brent-Ellis?' Karen Stannard asked, shading her eyes with concern.

'She's bearing up remarkably well,' Powell Frinton replied, a little stiffly. 'I saw her for a short while yesterday — Mr Brent-Ellis had taken various papers home and they needed to be returned, so I thought it best to call personally. Deliver my condolences.' He cleared his throat nervously. 'There's no immediate family, I understand, but various cousins were present, and everything is well in hand. And she is, of course, as we all know, a strong woman . . .' He was silent for a little while, peering down his narrow nose in thought, possibly mulling over the many clashes he had experienced with her as a councillor. 'You were both present at the occasion of this . . . ah . . . unfortunate occurrence, I understand.'

'I was still in the bar with some of the conference committee,' Karen Stannard replied quickly. 'I heard the commotion, but was unclear what it was all about. At the time, I didn't realize it involved Mr Brent-Ellis . . .'

The chief executive turned his pale eyes on Arnold. 'You were rather . . . closer to events, I gather.'

Arnold shrugged. 'I'd been for a late swim. I actually saw Mrs Brent-Ellis in the lobby, calling her husband's room. He must have ignored the phone . . . And I was heading for my room when I saw Mrs Brent-Ellis going into room 307 — I was along the same corridor as Mr Brent-Ellis — and when the screaming began I was the first there . . . But Mr Brent-Ellis was already dying, I think, when I got to his room.'

'Very sudden, a sad loss,' Powell Frinton murmured unconvincingly. He clicked his tongue in distaste. 'There'll be an inquest, of course, but it would appear that a heart attack . . . brought on by the stress of the situation . . . not that he had a history of heart problems.' He sniffed. 'He was a fairly active man, of course, time spent on the golf course . . .'

His voice died away. Arnold gained the impression the chief executive would have liked to discuss the matter further, discover what Arnold and Karen Stannard knew or thought about the whole business, but was too inhibited to ask such indelicate questions of his staff. Powell Frinton sucked his teeth and sighed.

'We now have a problem, of course. The department is not exactly overstaffed at the moment, and we will have to seek a replacement for the director. There's also the question of our further involvement in the archaeological conference . . .'

Karen Stannard leaned forward. 'I've already spoken to Colin Norfolk, the chairman of the conference committee. He seems determined that the conference shall proceed as planned. He's counting on our continued support.'

Powell Frinton's eyes widened at Karen Stannard's comment. 'In spite of the peculiar circumstances . . . ?' He grimaced. Clearly, the ways of the world were sometimes beyond his rather narrow, strait-laced conceptions of what constituted appropriate behaviour. 'Well, if the conference is to go ahead, we've already made our own commitments, so I suppose nothing much is lost . . . but if we *are* to continue our own involvement it might be seen as rather . . . heartless.'

Karen Stannard leaned forward, her eyes misty. 'I'm sure it's what Mr Brent-Ellis would have wanted . . . our continued involvement, I mean.'

Arnold stared at her. He was amazed at the insincerity of the demonstration. She had disliked Simon Brent-Ellis, and had had little time for his views on any subject, but now she appeared to be suggesting that they had been close enough for her to understand his feelings.

'As his deputy,' Powell Frinton remarked drily, 'I suppose you would know about such things.'

'I feel sure that he would have wanted our continued involvement,' she repeated firmly. 'The conference was dear to his heart — he saw it as bringing considerable kudos to the department and to the authority. And the planning is now at an advanced stage. To withdraw our support at such a time would be . . . well, it would cause problems.'

'Quite so,' Powell Frinton said in a disagreeable tone. 'Well, I've not had the opportunity to sound out members of the council yet, but it may well be they'll agree with your summation. Mrs Brent-Ellis may also have a view. *I* certainly will not cancel the arrangements made. I have no authority to do that. It's up to the members to decide, at the end of the day. But . . .' He shook his head. 'There are other important issues we must address, however. Not least the matter of Mr Brent-Ellis's successor.'

Karen Stannard flicked a quick glance in Arnold's direction and then sat up a little straighter in her chair. She crossed her slim legs, and raised one eyebrow, watching the chief executive intently.

'It goes without saying,' Powell Frinton intoned with little warmth in his voice, 'that as Mr Brent-Ellis's deputy, you, Miss Stannard, will now be asked to take over his duties. I imagine,' he added coolly, 'they will not be unfamiliar to you, and I feel certain you'll be able to ensure that the departmental work continues without any major interruption.' His lizard-cold eyes flickered to Arnold. 'You, Mr Landon, as the senior person after Miss Stannard, will also see some changes in your duties, I presume. But this will be a matter for discussion between you and Miss Stannard. I have no doubt,' he said, reverting to Karen Stannard, 'that you'll have some views about reorganization.'

'Yes, indeed,' Karen Stannard replied crisply, shedding any appearance of sorrow for the passing of Simon Brent-Ellis.

'There are certain weaknesses in the present structure within the department that I'd seek to rectify. Some of the duties that presently fall on various staff will need reassignment, and there are a number of issues I would wish to address—'

'I don't think you should go *too* far down the road of reorganization,' Powell Frinton warned unenthusiastically. 'We're not looking at a root-and-branch change here. I'm suggesting you consider only such changes as have been *forced* upon the department by reorganization as a result of the unfortunate death of Mr Brent-Ellis.'

'I understand that, but—'

'I mean *minimal* changes, Miss Stannard.'

There was a brief silence. Arnold noted the tension that had suddenly appeared in Karen Stannard's shoulders. She leaned forward in her chair, one elbow on her knee. 'I'm not sure that would be wise, Chief Executive. I don't wish to be critical of Mr Brent-Ellis now that he's dead, but the department had been allowed to . . . become rather loose and lacking in direction during his tenure. I would see it as a matter of duty to tighten things up, bring in new systems, reorganize work schedules and generally—'

'These things may well be necessary, Miss Stannard.' Powell Frinton cut in with a dismissive air, 'and you're to be commended for feeling changes are required. I myself have been of that opinion for some time. But I think issues such as these should be addressed only when Mr Brent-Ellis's successor has been placed in post.'

The silence grew around them, electrically. Karen Stannard's lips were set as she glared at the chief executive. 'But a few minutes ago, you said—'

Powell Frinton raised an elegant hand. 'I *said* that you would take over Mr Brent-Ellis's duties. By that, I meant until his successor is appointed. This is a stopgap measure, Miss Stannard. You surely did not expect to be immediately engaged as a replacement? The position of Director of the Department of Museums and Antiquities is classified as a senior-officer post. The authority regulations state quite specifically that all such posts are subject to external advertisement and interview. I have already instructed the clerks in the Legal Department to draw up the necessary newspaper advertisement and job description.' He smiled thinly. 'Now, I have no doubt that you would wish to apply, and that with the experience you've received as Mr Brent-Ellis's deputy, you would be a strong candidate for the job. But it is our duty to trawl for the best candidate, and I fully expect that there will be strong external competition.' His pale eyes shifted to Arnold. 'Indeed, there might be some others, apart from yourself, from within the authority, who would also wish to apply . . .'

Arnold returned to his room shortly afterwards, leaving Karen Stannard, white-faced and controlling her anger only with considerable effort, to continue her meeting with the chief executive, going over some points of immediate concern in the department. Arnold had managed to settle in behind his desk only for a matter of minutes before, with a groan, he realized that the office gossip, Jerry Picton, was eager to have a few words.

The man perched himself on the edge of Arnold's desk. Ungraciously, Arnold grunted, 'What do you want?'

'The full story, Arnold, what else?'

Picton's eager, weaselly features were marked with curiosity. Arnold stared at him with distaste. He didn't like Picton. The man had a capacity for mean-minded gossip and somehow it appeared in his face: a mean mouth, an unhealthy skin, narrow, intrusive eyes. And he seemed to clean his teeth rarely. 'All I can tell you is what the whole department has already guessed,' he said coldly. 'Miss Stannard will take over, temporarily, as director, until—'

'Hell, no, we all knew *that* was on the cards, Arnold! No, I want to know what really *happened* up there at that country club!' Jerry Picton leaned forward eagerly. 'Is it true . . . I mean, is it right what they're saying?'

'I've no idea what they're saying — whoever *they* are,' Arnold replied wearily.

'Well, you should know all about it — you were actually there, after all! The scuttlebutt is that Mrs Brent-Ellis went up to Amble because she was suspicious of her old man's shenanigans. They say she actually thought he was having it away with Karen Stannard! Crazy! I mean,' he scoffed, 'we all *know* how it is with her. Our deputy director would never take her knickers down for anyone in this department — or anyone of the *male* sex, anyway, is what I hear! Karen Stannard!'

'Now, look—'

'I mean, how wrong can you get? But the story is, Mrs Brent-Ellis went sneaking up there, suspicious because her husband had been away a couple of weekends with our Karen in tow, and expected to catch him finagling with her in some corner or other. And that's how she came to creep up to his room, burst in — and get the shock of her life. Not as big as his, of course!'

'I don't think we should be discussing this any further, Picton. I've got work—'

'But who would have believed *it* of old Brent-Ellis? I mean, we all thought he saw golf as a *substitute* for sex. Never imagined he'd have the gumption — let alone the courage — to jump into bed with someone other than his wife! Imagine it all, though,' Picton said almost dreamily 'You're there on the job, flailing away, and the old woman just bursts in on you . . . It's enough to give anyone a heart attack, particularly when the wife is someone like Councillor Eleanor Brent-Ellis. I mean, talk of brick houses, or blunt battle-axes . . . She must have scared the life out of him. But then, well . . . she *did*, didn't she?' he snickered.

Arnold pushed back his chair and rose to his feet. Quietly, but with a hint of menace in his tone, he said, 'I'm busy, Picton. I've no time for gossip. Out.'

Picton stood away from the desk. 'But you haven't told me who Brent-Ellis was with! I can't believe it was Karen Stannard — nobody believes that — but there's some doubt about exactly who was in the sack with him. Who was it he was banging, Arnold? Somebody reckons it was—'

'*Out!*'

The steely gleam in Arnold's eye persuaded Picton he was on dangerous ground. He backed away to the door and raised his hands. 'OK, you're busy, I'll talk to you again when you're in a more receptive mood—'

'Not on this topic, you won't,' Arnold snapped, and slammed the door in his face.

He went back to his desk angrily. He tried to settle down to some paperwork but Picton had brought back to his mind the scene when he had hurried along the corridor to Brent-Ellis's room: two women in hysterics, the naked, recumbent form of Brent-Ellis himself, already dying from a massive heart attack. Arnold had immediately rung for an ambulance, attempted to calm Mrs Brent-Ellis, wrapped a sheet around the sobbing woman beside the bed, and tried to organize the petrified hotel staff in an attempt to keep away curious guests from the spectacle in room 307. It had all seemed to happen so quickly thereafter — the noise, the confusion, the hotel manager wailing about the bad publicity, and finally the ambulance men and the police. He had tried to shut it out of his mind, but it kept returning, and worst of all in a sense was Mrs Brent-Ellis's white, shocked face and her continuous, repetitive, 'Why did he do it, the bastard, why did he do it?'

He stared blankly at the papers in front of him. The phone rang on his desk. It was Karen Stannard. She wanted to see him, immediately, in her office.

'He just dislikes women, that's the fact of it!' Karen Stannard snapped.

Arnold stared at her, realizing she was talking about the chief executive. Anger seemed to have made her even more beautiful if that was possible. Her eyes gleamed magnificently, the colour in her cheeks emphasized the elegant line of her facial bones, and the sheer animal magnetism that emanated from her emphasized her sexuality. She glared at him. 'Sit down, for God's sake. I want to talk to you!'

Arnold took a seat facing her. She had prepared carefully for her meeting with Powell Frinton. He would have appreciated her business-like appearance, in dark-grey suit, but she had probably got it wrong the way its generous cut revealed a white blouse, open at the throat, plunging at the neckline to enhance the swell of her breasts. Arnold could see how anger still stirred her bosom, but if she had thought her femininity would have influenced the chief executive, it had been a clear miscalculation on her part.

'He dislikes women, and he never wanted me to get this job, right from the start. He was at my first interview, you know, and I had a feeling then that he'd do all he could to influence the committee! But he missed out on that occasion, and I'll make damned sure he'll miss out again this time! There are cards I can play. Some of the councillors—' She cut herself off short, flickering a suspicious glance at Arnold, realizing she might say too much. 'And then there's that suspension they placed on me last year. You think that's influenced him?'

Arnold shook his head. 'I think Powell Frinton is just following the rules. He's a strait-laced lawyer. I don't believe there's anything personal in it.'

'You're always so bloody *rational*, Landon!' she exclaimed testily. She picked up a pencil from her desk, and threw it down again after a moment. She was silent for a little while, still fuming. 'And then there's this other thing . . .'

'Other thing?'

'You know — the submission for the Lottery grant. I couldn't *believe* it when Tom Patrick argued the other week that it should be given to an outside consultant! Do they all think me incapable, for God's sake? No, it's just because I'm a woman! Well, it's going to cost them, that's all I can say!'

'Has there been any movement on that front?' Arnold asked carefully, unwilling to get embroiled in the thrust of her argument.

'Faster than you'd have thought possible,' she grumbled. 'Tom Patrick has already drawn up a shortlist of three. Ritchie — and he's an *internal* candidate, in spite of what Patrick was saying — someone called Harrison, and an ex-journalist by the name of O'Hara. They're intending to interview on Friday. But no women, you'll notice, no women!' She groaned in despair. 'This authority . . .'

'They've certainly moved quickly,' Arnold agreed diplomatically.

'Mmm . . .' Karen Stannard seemed unsettled, a little wary. She hesitated, eyeing him suspiciously. 'You didn't appear all that enthusiastic about our continued involvement with the SPA conference.'

Arnold shrugged. 'It's as Powell Frinton intimated. It could be seen as somewhat disrespectful, in the circumstances . . .'

'Brent-Ellis almost saw this department down the drain with his incompetency,' she snapped. 'There's no reason why he should continue to do so by dying.'

Arnold was silent. He could guess why she had argued for the continued involvement. The SPA conference would be a platform for her — national exposure in her field of activity. It would help in her attempt to obtain Brent-Ellis's job.

There was still a measure of uncertainty in her glance. There was a short silence in the room. At last, almost reluctantly, she said, 'We . . . we've not had an opportunity to talk over . . . what happened at the country club.'

'No.'

'It was a complete surprise to me,' she said slowly. 'I mean, I can usually see the signs — I get enough signals sent in my own direction . . .'

He could believe it.

'But Brent-Ellis! I never thought he'd had it in him to stray! He was so terrified of his wife. And as for the woman he picked . . .'

Arnold recalled the image of the naked, screaming woman he had found in room 307. Karen Stannard was shaking her head.

'Sheila Norfolk! I know there was a problem between her and her husband — I picked up more than a couple of hints about the nature of the problem while he was talking to me at dinner. He's clearly a womanizer. But Sheila Norfolk . . . I can only guess that she wanted to get her own back on him. But her *choice* . . . I mean, Simon Brent-Ellis was not exactly the young girl's dream, was he? Or the middle-aged, rejected woman's, either. Don't you think so?'

Arnold shrugged. 'I don't see that it makes any difference. It happened . . . as to why, or how it happened, it makes little difference now.'

She sighed, shook her head and almost managed a rueful smile. 'You're so bloody *balanced*, you know? Never seem to be curious, don't like gossip, appear to tread the line that's right without being moralistic, never get in a rage. I don't bloody well trust you, Landon — I never have. You puzzle me sometimes when you do things which seem to me to be out of the character I perceive, but that only makes me distrust you more.' She paused, waiting. 'And even my saying *this* doesn't make you react.'

'You're entitled to your own opinion,' he said a little stiffly, more annoyed than he was prepared to admit.

She gave him a feline smile. She had perfect teeth. 'I think I do detect a little annoyance . . . Never mind.' She picked up the pencil again, toyed with it between slender fingers. 'I gathered from Powell Frinton that they'll proceed quickly to advertisement for the director's job. But I should be in post as acting director for several weeks — and even if someone else is finally appointed, there'll be a period in which I'll still be in charge. And during that time, whatever the chief executive says, I intend to bring in changes. And I'll expect you, as the senior officer under me, to support me to the hilt.'

'Of course.'

She stared at him, suspicion staining her glance. 'Your own position will naturally carry more responsibility. And if you prove to be up to it . . . there's no reason, after I get the job, why you shouldn't continue to carry such responsibility.'

Arnold waited. He could guess what was coming. It would be the real reason why she had called him to her office.

'And I *will* get the job, you know,' she said silkily. 'I'm pretty sure I can see off any opposition that's raised. Externally . . . and internally. I'll be frank with you, Arnold, there have been times when we've not seen eye to eye. Maybe I've been wrong about you — and I have to admit that when I was suspended last year, you behaved in a way that surprised me . . . you supported me. I'm . . .' She struggled for the words, avoiding his eye. 'I'm grateful for that. But I don't believe you could handle the post of director. Powell Frinton seemed to me to be giving you a push — but I wouldn't take the step if I were you, because if you apply for the job, and get shortlisted, you still won't come through at the end.'

She raised her head. Her eyes were tawny in colour, almost feral. 'And if you *did* apply for the job, I wouldn't be happy. It would look to me like disloyalty. And that could . . . affect our relationship, after I become director. Do I make myself clear?'

'Bell-like Miss Stannard.' Arnold smiled thinly. 'But let me put your mind at ease. I've no intention of applying for the job — not because of issues of disloyalty or because I don't want to *upset* you. I don't want the job. I've no desire to be head of this department. I enjoy what I do at the moment, it suits me. The politicking that's necessarily tied to the director's post, dealing with members, working with the chief executive and the other directors on policy matters, that doesn't appeal to me. I'm happy where I am. I don't intend to apply. You've no cause to worry.'

'I'm not *worried*, Landon,' she snapped curtly. 'I'm merely . . . clarifying a position. And I think I guessed this is the way you'd feel. But with Powell Frinton pushing you . . . I just thought you might get a rush of blood to the head and make a fool of yourself. After all, you have no academic qualifications, and you've hardly shown yourself to be ambitious . . . Your application would come a poor second to mine. But I'd like to make things absolutely clear. You don't stand a chance for the job. But I'd like you to give me an assurance—'

'Assurance?'

'That you won't be applying for the job, in opposition to me. One internal candidate is enough.'

'It's not a question of assurances,' Arnold replied, a little nettled. 'I'm just not interested in the job.'

She stared at him, unwilling to take his word for it. She gnawed at her perfect lower lip, considering the matter. 'I'm not sure I believe you.'

'That's a matter of indifference to me,' he replied shortly. 'I repeat, I'm not interested in the job.'

And with that she would have to be satisfied.

2

'I thought it would be useful if you met Mr O'Hara immediately,' Tom Patrick said in Arnold's office.

Steve O'Hara was of middle height, late thirties, sparely
built, with a mop of curly reddish hair and an engaging personality. He seemed a bouncy character: his face was cheerful
and freckled, his nose slightly snubbed, and his grin broad
and infectious. He had a Dublin accent and he played on
it, emphasizing its cadences, a stage Irishman, but there
was sharpness in his glance as he was introduced to Arnold,
weighing him up, that made Arnold suspect that O'Hara
would have perceptive depths that he kept cloaked and hidden by his cheerful, extrovert manner.

'So it's you who'll be the man to work with,' O'Hara
said, extending his hand. 'I've already met Miss Stannard,
but she informs me that with her new duties as head of the
department, she'll not have too much time herself to spend
on the Lottery submission now. So you're the unfortunate
man, it seems.'

Standing beside O'Hara, Councillor Patrick smiled edgily. He would have a view about Karen Stannard's no doubt
frosty reception of the consultant, Arnold guessed. 'We only
completed the interviews this afternoon,' Patrick said, 'but

rather than have Mr O'Hara make another trip from York to meet you, I thought it best to bring him in right away.' He glanced briefly at the Irishman. 'It was a hard-fought battle . . . we had three good candidates at the interview, but Mr O'Hara won through because of his knowledge and enthusiasm. He has extensive journalistic experience in Yorkshire and in London, he has impressive contacts, he's worked in the youth-training field for a while — and all this after training initially as an accountant. We're expecting big things of him.'

Arnold seemed to detect an oddly defensive note in Tom Patrick's voice.

'Well, the final pudding'll be as good as the ingredients we can put in, wouldn't you say, Mr Landon?' O'Hara was in a good humour, as he clapped Tom Patrick on the back in a gesture of familiarity, making the councillor wince slightly, and force a thin-edged smile. 'Mr Patrick here, now, he's had the good sense to offer me the job, but it's on you I'll be depending, Mr Landon, to set me on the right track, talk to the right people, and help me write the best kind of submission.'

'To that end, I think it would be a good idea if you were to introduce Mr O'Hara to the people up at Stangrove as soon as possible.' Tom Patrick moved slightly away from O'Hara's hand, still resting lightly on his shoulder. 'We'll need to be given a complete understanding of the site possibilities — though we do, of course, have Miss Stannard's notes.'

Which she would have relinquished with a bad grace, Arnold was sure. 'I can certainly make the introductions, but I'm afraid I'm a bit tied up at the moment — I won't be able to go up to the site for a few days.'

'Sure, that's no problem at all,' O'Hara grinned. 'I've some loose ends to tie up meself, in York — just let me know when we can start and I'll be up here to join you like a greyhound out of a trap.'

'Right,' Councillor Patrick said uneasily, inspecting his cuffs. 'Well, in that case I think I can leave it to you two to sort things out in due course. I would remind you both there's a certain urgency about this — the sooner we get the submission in the better. But for now — I guess we'd better tie up the contractual ends. Shall we go along to the chief executive's office, O'Hara?'

'To be sure, where a man with the name of Patrick leads, what's an O'Hara to do but follow?'

Arnold had the feeling that if he were to spend a great deal of time in the new consultant's company, the stagey Irishness of the man would prove to be somewhat wearing.

After the two men had left, Arnold began to bring up to date his notes on the file Karen Stannard had given him concerning Stangrove. He spent a little while poring over the four enclosures delineated on the map. The first, which had revealed the ceremonial cremation, was set a little aside from the others, in a more exposed position on the ridge, and he began to get the feeling that it did not really form part of the same sequence. The other three were more tightly grouped, though each within the general enclosure and ditch. The excavated tomb seemed to have been set at the edge, its northern limit actually breaking the line of the enclosure. It suggested to Arnold that its dating could be different. It was something he would have to discuss with George Pym, when next he visited the site.

He became aware there was someone standing at the door. For a dread moment he thought it might be Jerry Picton again, and he looked up sharply. It was not Picton, however, it was Chad Ritchie, who worked in the Planning Department. He had been one of the three shortlisted candidates for the consultancy. His long, serious features were somewhat woebegone. 'I guess you've heard, Arnold. I didn't get it.'

'I've just met the successful candidate.'

'What did you think of him?'

Arnold hesitated. 'I only met him briefly. I think he might be . . . noisy.'

'Made enough noise to convince the committee, anyway. I'm disappointed, Arnold, I have to admit. I thought my credentials were sound. I was looking forward to a bit of a break from the Planning Department.'

Arnold knew what he meant. It was the Planning Department in which Arnold himself had begun his career at Morpeth. 'I think the odds were always against you, Chad,' he said sympathetically. 'I think the committee was always intent on appointing an outside consultant. As an internal candidate, you weren't really what they wanted.'

'I suppose so,' Ritchie said gloomily. 'But it was all a bit odd. To be honest, my money was on the other guy — Harrison. He's got a track record — involved in two other submissions over the last couple of years. O'Hara, now, from what I gathered talking to him, he's never written a submission. He's been an accountant, a trainer, a journalist — jack of all trades, you might say, and he's had little or no experience of archaeology.' He eyed Arnold mournfully. 'Not like you and me.'

Ritchie's experience in the field was minimal, but Arnold did not say so. 'Perhaps it's the journalistic experience which swung the interviewing panel his way. Who's to say? You know what panels are like — they often go for a compromise candidate.'

Ritchie nodded in lugubrious fashion. 'Aye, I suppose so, but I could have done with the secondment, and the money . . . they're paying a handsome consultancy fee. And, I don't know, I had a funny feeling about the whole thing. I was talking to Harrison about it, and he got the same impression. O'Hara was very bouncy about the whole thing, very confident even before the interviews took place. It's as though he was expecting to get the job. As though it was all sewn up from the beginning.'

'He was just being Irish,' Arnold suggested drily.

* * *

It was over a week before Arnold was able to take O'Hara to the Stangrove site. The consultant chattered almost all the way, reeling off a string of Irish jokes, mainly about horse-racing. 'Did you hear the one about the owner whose horse for ever veered to the left when it came to the winning post, and allowed others to rush past him? The vet advised him to put a small piece of lead in the horse's ear and that would cure him. "How do I put it in?" the owner asked. "To be sure, with a gun," said the vet. Ha ha — do you get it?'

For a while it was amusing enough, but Arnold's patience finally became somewhat ragged with the incessant good humour. Cheerful, personable and friendly Steve O'Hara might be, but he could be wearing, and Arnold was still left with the impression that the man had gained the habit of talking interminably as a method of cover for his real personality. It was all a show, a deliberate performance to hide a reality. Arnold doubted whether it was a matter of insecurity. Rather, he guessed it might be that O'Hara was out to make an impression, persuade those who listened to him that he was merely a bouncy buffoon, whereas in practice the truth was probably quite different.

They arrived at the site about eleven in the morning. George Pym was there alone. Sue Lawrence and Paul Samuels had gone into the village to get some provisions, so the three men had the opportunity to sit down and allow George to explain the nature of the site, and the hopes they had for it. O'Hara listened with apparent interest and made extensive notes in shorthand — he still managed to present the amiable Irish exterior, but when he concentrated much of it fell away, and it was clear to Arnold that the man was indeed using the extrovert personality as a protective shellac. He had a sharp, intelligent mind and, Arnold suspected, a mental toughness. As a journalist he would have needed that.

Over coffee, when George Pym had finished his explanation, Arnold raised the matter of the enclosures. 'You know, I've got the feeling that there's a distinction between the grave you've excavated and the other three. I suspect the others are much older — they've been dug in a more protected area, almost prime sites, you might say. The cremation grave, I think it may well have been the result of a different culture from the others — much later in time.'

'Are you suggesting there's a chance it won't be a cremation in the other enclosures? That maybe we'll have a more interesting find on our hands?'

'It's possible,' Arnold said carefully. 'You're more expert than I, but I have a gut feeling—'

'If you could find something dramatic, I could build it into the submission, strengthen the proposal,' O'Hara cut in.

Arnold hesitated. 'It's your site, George, and I don't know what your plans are for the immediate future—'

George Pym shrugged his burly shoulders. 'Things have slowed down, really. The funding's dried up, as you know, we've released those youngsters from the training agency. Paul and Sue have their teaching schedules, so their time will be limited . . . I hadn't really planned on anything major until we could see where the money was coming from. And that's down to Mr O'Hara, really.'

'And Alan Farmer,' Arnold murmured. 'But I was thinking . . . if it would help, I have my weekends, and a couple of days' leave are due to me — I'd be more than happy to come up here and do some work.'

George Pym smiled. 'That would be really great! Any extra hands would be welcome. But what would you have in mind?'

Arnold pulled forward the site drawings. 'Well, you've opened up the cremation tomb — we can leave that to one side now. But these other three enclosures — as you'll see, O'Hara, there's this large one here at the corner. Then a little below and set aside, there's this small one, then a third rather differently shaped enclosure below the ridge. With limited resources we clearly can't attempt anything major . . . but I'd like to suggest, George, that we take a crack at this enclosure here — take off the topsoil, maybe run in an exploratory trench, and see if it really is a grave . . .'

George Pym was enthusiastic. He clenched and unclenched a powerful fist. 'I think that would be a good idea. We won't be able to get very far . . .'

'I'll be taking O'Hara down to meet Alan Farmer later this morning,' Arnold said. 'Who knows? Maybe he'll be prepared to help us out, pay for a small team to be brought in, get some earth-shifting equipment . . .'

They huddled over the drawings while O'Hara continued to make notes. They were hardly aware of the arrival at the site of the other members of the team, until they actually entered the hut. Sue Lawrence came in first, dumping her purchases on the small table behind the hut door. She turned, beginning to remove her jacket. 'We managed to get all we wanted except the—'

The words died on her lips as she caught sight of the man with Arnold and George Pym. Slowly the colour drained from her face. Her tall, rangy figure was rigid as she stood staring at O'Hara. He pushed back his chair and rose to his feet. He was grinning mischievously. 'By all that's holy, Sunday Susan, my favourite girl! I hadn't realized you were working on this project — say now, how long has it been?'

He came forward as though to embrace her but she put her hands up, and he stopped. They stood facing each other, much of a height, and he spread his arms wide, mockingly. 'Now don't say you're not pleased to see me!'

She had no time to reply. Behind her, Paul Samuels stepped into the doorway. He seemed thunderstruck for a moment, then his belligerent features slowly turned red. He ran an angry hand over his short-cropped skull and glowered. 'O'Hara! What the hell are you doing here?'

'Ah, the fighting turkey cock!' O'Hara beamed satirically. 'We've got quite a little reunion here, haven't we?'

George Pym stood up, nonplussed, staring at the three of them. 'You all know each other?'

Sue Lawrence ignored him. She stood almost hugging herself, arms wrapped across her breast, but Paul Samuels pushed forward, bristling with anger, eyes aflame. 'What's going on here? Why is O'Hara here?'

The Irishman grinned, unabashed. 'Legitimately, little man, legitimately. And as always, just to help.'

'Help what? Destroy, more like! What are you after, O'Hara? What's here for you to rip off?'

George Pym moved forward, big, clumsy, not understanding the tension in the hut, but placating in his manner. He raised a beefy hand. 'Mr O'Hara has been taken on as a consultant, to write the submission for the Lottery grant. He's here to get an understanding of the—'

'You must all be crazy!' Paul Samuels snarled. 'This journalistic guttersnipe—'

'*Paul*!' O'Hara stepped forward, still smiling, but the smile was hard-edged. He brushed past Sue Lawrence, who almost stumbled to avoid him, and he took Paul Samuels by the elbow, steering him away towards the door. 'I think you and I had better step out here. If you have things to say to me, they're better said in private.'

'Damn you, what I've got to say—'

'In private, my friend!'

The Irishman propelled the angry little man outside the hut. Arnold looked at Sue Lawrence. She still appeared shaken, but was re-gathering her composure. She avoided his eyes. George Pym turned to her, in puzzlement. 'What the hell's going on?'

Dumbly, she shook her head, and turned aside to start unpacking the provisions she had bought.

George Pym glanced helplessly at Arnold, and then switched his attention back to the young woman 'Sue, leave that for a moment. What on earth's the problem here? You know this man? He's here to work with us, help us with the submission, but if you've got a difficulty—'

She shook her head again, and raised her chin, almost defiantly, her eyes glittering with determination. 'No, George, there's no problem as far as I'm concerned. I know . . . I knew O'Hara. But that's all in the past.' She swallowed hard. 'I'm surprised you've never come across him yourself, but I suppose you've been away so much from the university . . . It was just a shock, seeing him standing here . . .'

'Sue, are you sure you're all right?' Pym asked solicitously. He was a big man, but his hand was gentle on her arm, his eyes troubled and anxious. When she nodded, he turned and glanced at Arnold. 'Maybe a coffee . . . ?'

Arnold nodded and walked across to the percolator which was kept constantly bubbling. He poured her a cup. She sat down, still pale, but more composed. 'So,' she said, smiling with a forced brightness, and gesturing towards the site map, 'you've been planning something?'

'Arnold's suggesting we start opening up the enclosure, dig in a trench,' Pym replied after a moment, watching her carefully. With a barely subdued anxiety he brought her up to date with the conversation they had been having. She nodded with a forced enthusiasm, her mind clearly still on other things. Before he had finished, however, Steve O'Hara returned to the hut. He was alone.

'Now that was a wild whirring antic, wasn't it! My old mother used to say that bygones should be bygones — that was just before she pushed me father under a truck — but there's those who don't hold to those views.' He grinned slyly at Sue Lawrence. 'But Sunday Susan doesn't bear grudges, now does she? Not like young Paul there, it seems. But I've had a word with him, persuaded him of his error, because I'm just the happy soul of the party and nothing else! The rider to the rescue of this project! So though he's still smarting about days gone by, and mutual misunderstandings, I've cooled him down a bit. He's off to sulk somewhere on the site, but he'll come round in time.'

'What's the problem between you?' George Pym asked reluctantly.

'Problem?' O'Hara laughed delightedly and scratched his head. 'There's no problem as far as I'm concerned. Paul and I, we had our little differences a year or so ago, and it's a sad thing that it's still a problem for him. It's in other hands, anyway, so he should be forgetting it. Like my Sunday Susan here. I can see there's no begrudging in those beautiful eyes.'

There was a hint of annoyance staining George Pym's tone. 'We work well together here — I don't want disruptions—'

'And you'll get none,' O'Hara interrupted cheerfully, turning away from Sue Lawrence. 'I've now heard what you have to say about the site and its possibilities. I've got a copy of the drawings. I don't need to be coming up here disturbing you in your work. No disruption, George, none at all. In fact,' he added, turning to Arnold, 'there's no reason why we shouldn't call it a day here now. Time to go meet Mr Farmer, I'd have thought.'

It certainly was time, Arnold considered.

* * *

While they drove the two miles to Stangrove Hall, O'Hara was uncharacteristically silent. Whatever denial he might make of a difficulty between him and the two lecturers from York, Arnold was certain that he was mulling over what had happened at the dig site. But when they turned into the long drive of the hall, he cheered up, and when he was introduced to Alan Farmer he had donned the mask of bonhomie once again.

'It's a fine place you've acquired here, squire! I think only a man of means could afford a place this size!'

'The maintenance costs are high, certainly,' Farmer agreed.

'And that'll be a West Country accent I detect?'

'I'm from Exeter originally,' Alan Farmer replied, flicking a glance at Arnold from his pale-blue eyes. 'It's where I started my business.'

'And successfully so, it seems, if the hall is to be considered. And you'll be owning the land where the enclosures are,' O'Hara said. 'You'll not be keeping horses up here as well — a stud, maybe?'

'I've no great interest in horses.'

'And I'm quite the reverse. The nags have always been me passion, and badly they've served me at that . . . but then isn't that so for all Irishmen?' He waved his hand, taking in the furnishings of the broad, elegant drawing room. 'You'll not mind me saying, I hope, but you seem to be a relatively young man to be retiring and becoming a philanthropist. What exactly was your line?'

Farmer pinched his broken, lopsided nose between finger and thumb. He seemed a little put out by O'Hara's direct manner. 'Computer software.' He eyed the consultant warily. 'And yours?'

O'Hara laughed. 'Oh, a bit of this, bit of that . . . accountancy, training, journalism. And when I heard of this consultancy, well, I thought I'd try my hand. Another string to the bow, you understand. And some more cash to throwaway on the nags, if the truth be known.'

Farmer turned away to the sideboard. 'Drink? I've a good whisky here . . . So you have no archaeological experience, then, Mr O'Hara?'

Accepting the whisky, O'Hara shook his head. 'That's not entirely true. I've done a certain amount of writing about it. And there was a television programme . . .'

'Is that so?' Farmer said, handing Arnold his glass. 'I have an interest in a television production company myself.'

O'Hara nodded and sipped his whisky. Arnold thought he detected a mocking glint in the man's eyes as he held Farmer's glance. The owner of Stangrove Hall was perceptive enough, and after a moment he frowned as he stared at the Irishman. There was a slow dawning of recognition. 'Steven O'Hara . . . *Bonfire at Batavorum*. You wrote that programme . . . ?'

'I did, your honour, I cannot say a lie. Fame at last.' He grinned at Alan Farmer. 'Not that the programme's seen the light of day yet. And maybe never will — if certain people get their way. But I still would have thought a production company like yours would have had the guts to go on with it.'

'Not *my* production company, Mr O'Hara — I merely have a stake holding, and I'm only recently on the board. The decision had already been taken to halt production. So . . .'

He was still frowning slightly as he watched O'Hara smiling appreciatively at the amber liquid in his glass. 'You've caused the company a certain amount of trouble, it seems.'

'Not so,' O'Hara countered swiftly. 'It's other people have caused the trouble. I'm just an honest journeyman, trying to earn a crust. If other people don't have the nous to seize an opportunity when they see one, that's a problem of their own making.' He smiled engagingly. 'But all that's another story, as they say. I'm here to do something else entirely. Help you spend some of your money. I understand you'll be matching anything we can win from the Lottery fund.'

'I have reached an understanding of that nature with Miss Stannard, yes,' Farmer replied uncertainly. 'I'm prepared to put in some myself, and I think I can round up a few business acquaintances to get the rest.'

'Well, I'll have to see if I can help you in that little endeavour then, mustn't I?' O'Hara hesitated, raising a quizzical eyebrow. 'You'll be aware then that Paul Samuels is working up at the dig?'

Farmer nodded. 'But I hadn't made the connection—'

'No matter, it's of no consequence,' O'Hara said smoothly. 'It's all in the hands of the legal sharks now anyway, but there's the thought in me mind that just by going up to the site, well, it could be leading to certain tensions, and I *will* have to take another look at the place from time to time . . . And I don't think Morpeth is a base from which I can work at my best.' He flashed his teeth at Farmer, and glanced around the room. 'So I wonder whether I'd be able perhaps to use Stangrove Hall as a base to prepare the submission. You'll surely have a little cubbyhole in a grand place like this, where I could tuck myself away.'

Arnold was startled. The effrontery of the approach also clearly took Alan Farmer aback. He hesitated, his face looking more lopsided than ever as he considered the matter. O'Hara went on cheerfully, 'After all, it's all in the same good cause, isn't it? And Mr Landon — and Miss Stannard, of course — they'll then know where to find me.'

The mention of Karen Stannard's name gave their host pause for thought. His glance slipped away from them, and he gazed out of the windows reflectively. He sipped at his whisky, then shrugged. 'It will be for a short period only, I suppose, so . . . I think we can manage to give you a seat in the library, Mr O'Hara.'

'That's grand, Mr Farmer. And let me compliment you on your choice of the malt — I prefer the Irish meself, of course, but this is grand.' He beamed at his host and raised his glass. 'Grand it is, indeed.'

As he sipped at his own glass of whisky, Arnold hoped that Alan Farmer would not have reason to regret his hospitality. Farmer gestured to them to follow him, and he took them into the library. O'Hara expressed pleasure at its size and stock, and announced it would be a splendid place in which to work. While he wandered around the room, examining the books and running his hand along the long polished table in the centre, Arnold drew Alan Farmer to one side.

'I'm sorry about that. I hadn't intended, or realized—' Farmer smiled faintly. His narrow eyes were inexpressive. 'I was slightly taken aback when he asked to be . . . accommodated here. But it's of no great consequence. The library is little enough used.' He paused for a moment, uncharacteristically uncertain. 'So, you've taken over the management of the project from Miss Stannard now?'

Arnold nodded. 'She's had to take over as director of the department.' He hesitated. 'In managing the project from the county point of view, I've decided I'll try to spend some of my spare time at the dig.'

'That's good. So Miss Stannard won't be spending much time up here then?'

Arnold was aware of the slight strain in Farmer's tone, an attempt at casualness that was forced. 'Hardly any, I would think. She's going to be pretty busy at Morpeth . . . Meanwhile, George Pym and I feel that there's the possibility of an interesting find if we break open one of the other enclosures. It could be used to support the submission. But we won't be able to get very far in time unless we can get some additional financing . . .'

Alan Farmer drained his glass, as O'Hara came across to join them. 'I'd be happy to talk further to Miss Stannard at any time about our . . . present agreement. I'm sure if you tell me what you'll need, Mr Landon, we can come to a satisfactory arrangement. And . . . er . . . when you see Miss Stannard at the office, perhaps you could get her to ring me, so we can talk further about the financing — and any other ways in which I can assist the project . . .'

He turned to the Irishman. 'Will this be suitable accommodation then, Mr O'Hara?'

'It'll be fine to be sure. I'll start dumping me things here as soon as I can . . .'

3

Over the next two weekends Arnold worked at the site with George Pym. Neither Sue Lawrence nor Paul Samuels were available because of teaching commitments at the university, but Alan Farmer had been as good as his word, and had arranged for some earth-moving equipment to be made present on site, along with three young men who were paid to work at the dig under Pym's direction.

The work progressed well. When the topsoil had been stripped from the second, small enclosure it soon became clear that they were looking at a chambered burial. There was a ripple of excitement when the human femur was discovered below the layer of large stones, and then gradually as the rest of the skeleton was brushed clean of the clinging soil they realized that Arnold's guess had been correct. This burial had probably been undertaken at a date later than the cremation discovered earlier, so the likelihood was that the other two unexcavated areas would also be chambered burials.

'We can now see how the interment was undertaken,' George Pym explained to Alan Farmer when the owner of Stangrove Hall visited the site to check on their progress.

'They dug a square pit in the first instance — pits of this kind were dug, we believe, to allow the dead person to communicate with the underworld powers, the chthonic beings who inhabited regions deep below the earth. Then they constructed a ledge at the bottom of the pit so that one end was deeper than the rest. On the ledge they placed a long wooden box — effectively the coffin — in the deepest part of the grave, so that it fitted tightly across the end. There's no wood to be seen now, of course — the planks have long since rotted away, but we have the darker signs here in the earth deposits to show where the box was placed. The corpse was interred in the box, a crouched burial, legs drawn up almost in a foetal position and the box was covered with heavy stones—'

'Someone wanted to make sure he stayed down there, hey?' Alan Farmer said with a smile.

George Pym laughed. 'You're not too far out with that idea — the old ones were always concerned that the spirit of a dead person might get out and wander around. That's the reason for the stones, and also the enclosures and ditches. And with this one, maybe, particularly so.'

'Why was that?'

Arnold gestured across to the table in the hut. 'We found these implements scattered near the skeleton.' He recalled the shiver that had gone down his spine — part excitement, part reminder of ancient fears — when he recognized the implements for what they were. He walked across to the table. 'This one is a stylized representation of a raven, the traditional symbol of Donn, the sombre god of the dead from whom men were considered to have descended. Interesting, because of later Roman links — Dis Pater, the Roman lord of the underworld, is clearly linked to the Celtic death-god Donn. The Celts attached great significance to afterlife . . .'

'But what are these?' Farmer asked, as he gestured towards a small collection of bronze and iron objects.

'That's the fascinating thing,' George Pym replied, folding his arms and gazing contemplatively at the artefacts. 'Arnold scraped them out of the earth near the left hand of the skeleton. These two are iron — these copper alloy, and these rods were bronze. Altogether, they make up what we might call a basic surgical kit.'

'You're joking!'

Arnold shook his head, smiling. 'No, if you look closely, these two iron implements are really scalpels — this is a pair of forceps and this copper alloy implement is a scooped probe.'

Alan Farmer stared at him, his pale eyes wide with astonishment. 'But you've reckoned this site could be as much as three thousand years old! Yet you're talking about a doctor's grave — *surgical* implements!'

Arnold nodded. 'This find isn't unique. We're mistaken in assuming that surgical techniques only started in the period of recorded history. In Celtic times there was a wide range of surgical and medical treatments and relatively sophisticated surgical techniques which would have evolved over many generations. The Romans had them too — and before them, the Greeks. We've evidence of trepanning, for instance — to relieve pressure on the brain.'

'You amaze me. A *doctor*, two thousand years ago.'

'Well, probably something more than a doctor,' Arnold replied quietly. 'Rather, a shaman.'

'That's right,' George Pym intervened. 'Those men who learned surgical skills were feared and revered — they were regarded as magicians and their incantations would have been considered as important as their medical skills. It was all one and the same. The relief of pain — and the predictions of the future, it was all within their powers. The shamans were regarded as holy men for their skills—'

'And the presence of the raven in the tomb would suggest that this old man was reckoned to be in personal communication with the gods of the underworld.'

Alan Farmer shook his head, inspecting the implements carefully. 'So this site really is an important one.'

'We think so,' Arnold replied. 'Because if the shaman — a very important man — is buried here in this chambered tomb, what lies in the other two? We have a larger one in particular — my feeling is that the grouping of these tombs is important. The first one George opened up was different — a cremation of an earlier date, a different culture. But the others . . . they're grouped on the ridge in what was clearly regarded as a holy site, and I suspect they form a family burial, perhaps, or a group of courtiers, who knows?'

'We can make our guesses, once we've uncovered the tombs.'

'Fascinating,' Alan Farmer murmured.

They walked around the site again and pondered over the enclosures. Arnold listened as George Pym explained how the otherworld rites of ancient times could be complex and grim: ritual burials with heads or hands and feet missing. They could also sometimes reflect a belief in the afterlife with the burial of secular items such as pots, toilet accessories, martial equipment. 'But what is clear is that the burials of bodies in plank-lined chambers generally characterize a higher stratum of Celtic society, and that's why we're excited about this one.' George Pym's tanned features were flushed with enthusiasm. 'A shaman, near two other burials — who knows what we'll find on this site?'

Farmer mused over the possibilities opened up to him. He shook his head. '*Incredible* . . . This site must be kept open, the whole area must be worked on . . .'

'How's O'Hara getting on with the submission?' Arnold asked.

Alan Farmer shrugged. 'I can't say I've seen much of him at Stangrove Hall. He's been working in the library, but he stays out of my way well enough. He's got a pile of notes he keeps there in the drawer, so clearly he's building the submission up by reference to materials in the library as well as what's happening here. But I can't say how far he's got. Doesn't he make reports to Karen?'

Arnold noted the use of the first name. He had seen Alan Farmer in the office reception area at Morpeth a couple of times, and Jerry Picton had said it was rumoured that Karen Stannard was being 'squired' around by a country gentleman.

Not that he'd get much out of it, Picton had leered, in his view the man would be in for a shock if he tried to lay a finger on her. Arnold wasn't so sure — Picton's sour comments about Karen Stannard's sexual predilections could be well wide of the mark. They had grown out of a significant lack of success from would-be Lotharios at county hall, who could be seeking an explanation for their failures.

In reply to Farmer, Arnold nodded. 'Yes, he'll be reporting to Miss Stannard, I imagine. She services the committee that Councillor Patrick has formed to oversee the Lottery submission. In fact, there's a meeting tomorrow night. I've been called to stand by in case I'm needed . . .'

* * *

Which was very much a waste of time, he decided, as he worked late in his office the following evening. He was able to get on with some paperwork while he waited, but when it was finished he was effectively just sitting there with nothing to do, except think. His mind drifted to the death of the director and he wondered how Mrs Brent-Ellis was coping with her loss. She was a strong woman, who had dominated her husband, and she would miss that, he had no doubt. Arnold had held Simon Brent-Ellis in little regard, but he had not been a malicious man, merely a weak, incompetent one. Arnold was still surprised by the man's boldness in having an affair with Sheila Norfolk, however — he had always regarded Brent-Ellis as being completely under his wife's thumb. It was a boldness which had killed him, nevertheless.

At eight o'clock there was a tap on his door. It was Alan Farmer, dark-suited, white shirt and sober tie. 'Hello, Landon. The committee still in session?'

'That's right. And I'm still waiting for the call, which I suspect won't now materialize. They shouldn't be too much longer. Can I help you?'

Farmer smiled. 'No, I'm waiting for Karen, really. I'd arranged to take her out to dinner this evening, had a table booked for eight-fifteen. Looks like we're going to be a bit late . . . Mind if I take a seat?'

'Be my guest. I've finished any work I need to do tonight.' Farmer dragged a chair forward and sat down. 'Will you be attending the SPA conference? I've had an invitation, of course, but I won't know many faces there—'

'We'll be there in force.' Arnold assured him. 'George Pym, Sue Lawrence, Paul Samuels and I, as well as Miss Stannard . . . The conference is a prestigious one, there'll be some excellent papers delivered from experts. Even the chief executive is now in favour of it — though he's probably had his arm twisted by the members of the council who see it as an opportunity for junketing.'

Alan Farmer laughed, it made him look considerably younger. 'Well, there's that possibility, of course. I understand some book publishers have been prevailed upon to hold a cocktail reception at the commencement of the conference, and there'll be wine at the dinner, naturally. They'll have their chance.' He paused, as he became aware of someone walking down the corridor. 'That sounds like Karen.'

So he was attuned to the pace of her step, Arnold mused.

He stood up as the door opened and Karen Stannard appeared in the doorway. Since she was being taken out to dinner, she had made some concessions to her normally formal wear in the office. She was wearing a dark-green dress which clung to her figure, high-necked, but emphasizing the curves of her body. Farmer's eyes were shining with admiration as he looked at her. 'All finished?' he asked eagerly.

She hesitated, stared at him vaguely for a moment, as though her mind was on other things. 'Alan I thought you'd be waiting downstairs . . . No, I'm sorry . . . the committee meeting is over—'

'Everything resolved?' Farmer asked.

'What?' She seemed confused, as though something was bothering her. A little impatiently, she went on, 'No, not exactly. O'Hara put in his submission and report and it was very well received.' Her eyes glowed greenly with a barely veiled resentment. 'Tom Patrick went a bit over the top, if you ask me, but . . . anyway, O'Hara's been asked to put some finishing touches to the submission. I'll have to check it out, finally, and then it looks as though we'll be able to get it off to the Heritage people.' She hesitated, glancing at Arnold. 'No, the committee meeting is over, but Landon and I . . . we've been asked to go to the chief executive's office. So, I'm afraid it's more delay, Alan. If you like, you could cancel this evening, and we'll make it another time—'

'Not at all,' he hastened. 'I can ring them at the restaurant, warn them we'll be late. It'll be no problem.'

She gave him a warm smile, and yet there was something lacking in it. She glanced at Arnold again, there was a strange calculation in her eyes. It was possible she was a little disturbed that Farmer had been sitting here in Arnold's office, and that Arnold clearly knew she and Farmer were going out to dinner. It was none of his affair, of course, but he gained the impression she was somewhat displeased. On the other hand, it could be something else entirely. He had never been able to read Karen Stannard.

'Yes . . .' she said hesitantly. 'Well, will you wait here, Alan, or downstairs?'

'I'll go down to reception.'

'I don't think we'll be long. Landon, shall we go?' Arnold walked down the corridor with her towards Powell Frinton's office. Her back was stiff, she seemed lost in thought and she did not look at him. As they neared the office, she suddenly snapped, 'He's a nice man.'

'I agree.'

'But rather . . . intense.'

'I wouldn't know about that.'

'He can be very useful to us, in the department.'

Arnold wondered whether that was the only reason why she was going out with him to dinner.

When they entered Powell Frinton's office, Arnold was surprised to see that Councillor Patrick was also there. The two men were seated away from the desk, near the boardroom table that took up part of his large office. Powell Frinton rose and suggested they take seats at the table. Arnold noted that he had a glass of sherry in his hand, while Tom Patrick was sipping whisky in a cut-glass tumbler. The chief executive was clearly extending hospitality to the councillor after a long committee meeting, he did not extend the courtesy to the new arrivals.

Tom Patrick's heavy eyebrows were knitted in thought, but there was a hesitancy in his glance, as though he felt uncertain of his ground under Powell Frinton's eye. He leaned forward, one elbow on the table. 'You weren't at the meeting, Mr Landon, so I should bring you up to date. O'Hara has turned in a first-class piece of work — splendid submission, quite up to the standard we were hoping for. There's just a few bits and bobs he needs to do to complete things—' Patrick glanced at Karen Stannard — 'for which we're grateful to the acting director. They were valid points you made, Miss Stannard.'

She nodded, but made no reply. Arnold could guess what she was thinking — that she could have completed just as good a submission herself. Powell Frinton was leaning back in his chair, twirling the half-empty glass of sherry between the fingers of his right hand. 'It's expected that the submission should be complete in a few days, and then it can be sent off immediately.'

'And I'm pretty sure it'll turn out to be successful. The whole committee was most impressed with O'Hara's work,' Councillor Patrick repeated emphatically. Powell Frinton sniffed.

Karen Stannard shifted slightly in her seat. Arnold wondered whether she was still smarting from the employment of the Irish consultant.

'Is there anything new to report from the site?' Tom Patrick asked. 'Anything that can be added to the submission to make it more effective?'

'We've opened up another burial tomb,' Arnold replied, and received a flashing look from Karen Stannard, annoyed that she had not been told first. He went on to explain its importance and Patrick nodded enthusiastically.

'Excellent, excellent. This gives me even higher hopes of the submission. Can you do a report quickly, get it to O'Hara? He's working up at Stangrove Hall, I understand.'

Arnold agreed to do so and there was a short silence. Powell Frinton slowly finished his sherry and found something absorbing in his veined hands; Tom Patrick stared at his whisky glass. The silence grew around them. The chief executive seemed reluctant to move on. He pinched his nostrils between finger and thumb and frowned.

'You . . . ah . . . you won't be aware that there was a meeting of Councillor Tremain's finance committee before we held the grant sub-committee meeting this evening, under the chairmanship of Mr Patrick . . . The details need not concern us here and now, except that it's been stressed to us that the financial position of the authority is indeed quite grave and it's necessary for us to . . .ah . . .'

'Pull in our belts,' Patrick supplied.

Powell Frinton did not care for the phrase and wrinkled his nose in displeasure. 'In those circumstances there was considerable discussion of the situation following from the sad demise of Mr Brent-Ellis . . . The fact is, the vacancy created does give us an opportunity to save a little money, and every little bit helps . . . Of course, we're bound by standing orders to advertise the post in order to get a good standard of application, but it is now felt that it might perhaps not be necessary to go through the whole advertising process after all . . .'

The silence was heavy, suddenly. Powell Frinton's features were like granite in their clear disapproval of what he, as an officer of the authority, was being forced to say. Tom Patrick broke the silence, doggedly. 'There is a way around it,' he said.

Karen Stannard sat up a little straighter, hanging on every word. Arnold suddenly realized what she was thinking: if they intended to save money on advertising, they might also wish to save money by making an internal appointment. They could simply confirm her in office.

'It was, in fact, Mr Patrick here who came up with a proposal which the finance committee was happy to endorse. And since it concerns both of you, I thought it best to call you in here, with Mr Patrick, to let you know how we intend to proceed.' Powell Frinton hesitated. He was clearly uneasy, unhappy at the process he was about to describe. He was a stickler for the proprieties, a lawyer who had been brought up to consider rules and regulations as sacrosanct. 'In the first instance, we've decided to delay the appointment itself for three months. Miss Stannard will continue in post during that period but will consult me on the reorganization of the duties, sharing them with you, Mr Landon. Miss Stannard will therefore continue, in the near future, as acting director of the department.'

It should have been what she wanted to hear, but from the tone in his voice she felt there was something wrong. She was tense, and she was aware that somehow or other a decision had been reached which would not please her. Arnold sensed it, and yet could not think what the problem was.

'The decision to ask you both to hold the fort, of course, means that we need not advertise. And in the meanwhile, it is felt that perhaps in the interests of economy, since we can already see an effective shortlist being drawn up without advertisement, interviews will be held in three months' time with . . . ah . . . selected candidates.' Powell Frinton's cold glance rested on her. 'Miss Stannard, you will of course be one of those candidates.'

She inclined her head gracefully, but her eyes were suspicious, knowing there was more to come.

'Secondly, the committee was very impressed by the work undertaken by Mr O'Hara. He is not, of course, the kind of . . . professional we would normally expect to see coming forward' Powell Frinton's mouth seemed somewhat white around the edges as he went on—'but the committee feel that they would like to see his contract extended somewhat so that he might get a better . . . ah . . . flavour of the work in the department. After which, on conclusion of the three months, he would be added to the shortlist in contention with Miss Stannard.'

The room was still. Arnold could see that Powell Frinton was unhappy at the shortlisting decision the committee had made; Tom Patrick sat staring at his whisky glass, listening intently.

Karen Stannard leaned forward. There was a hint of frost in her tone. 'Are you saying, Chief Executive, that during this three months Mr O'Hara's contract will be extended and he will be assigned to work in the department?'

'The departmental vacancy exists, as a consequence of Mr Brent-Ellis's demise. His consultancy fees can therefore be debited from the department. And . . . the committee feels that it would be the . . . ah . . . most appropriate way to give Mr O'Hara the necessary understanding of the work of the department, and experience to fit him for interview.'

She opened her mouth to snap a sharp reply to the chief executive but thought better of it. She laced her fingers in front of her on the table. Her knuckles were white with suppressed anger.

Aware of her annoyance, and possibly sympathizing with it, Powell Frinton turned to Arnold. 'It will be necessary that Miss Stannard takes Mr O'Hara under her wing, Mr Landon. But that means more must therefore devolve on you. You will act as deputy to Miss Stannard. She will take the major responsibilities with your assistance. And Mr O'Hara will . . . shadow Miss Stannard, I think was how Mr Patrick described it. Would that be the correct management term, sir?'

Tom Patrick's glance was sharp. He detected the disapproving sneer in Powell Frinton's tone. 'It is.'

'And then, at the end of the three-month period,' Powell Frinton continued, 'the committee has decided that you, Mr Landon, will make the third candidate for the interviews and will be required to present yourself for interview for the position of director of the department. Which will not otherwise be advertised to open competition.'

Stunned, Arnold was unable to say a word.

* * *

'You *bastard*! You told me you weren't *interested* in the job,' Karen Stannard raged. 'You said you wouldn't be applying! I made it clear to you—'

'And I'm making it just as clear to you,' Arnold intervened angrily, facing her in her office, 'that this has been none of my doing. I told you the truth. I don't want the job. And I've made no application—'

She waved a hand angrily. 'Application be damned! You didn't say anything when that cold snake told you that you were going to be shortlisted! Why the hell didn't you pull out then?'

'Because I was taken aback, and it wasn't the place to do so, or have an argument in front of Tom Patrick! Don't worry, I intend to see Powell Frinton privately and explain to him that I have no intention of taking the job.'

'I don't believe you!'

'Now, look—'

'This is all a plot. I can see through all you slimy bastards so clearly.' She was beside herself with anger, irrational, unable to listen, magnificent in her rage. 'It's all been fixed up behind closed doors. It's a conspiracy. They don't want me in the job because I'm a woman, because I show up then inefficiencies, and because they know I'm better than they are! They've resented me right from the beginning. That was behind the suspension last year . . . and it's behind this dirty trick now.' She paced the room, arms tightly folded across her breasts, working herself up to a feline fury, spitting and clawing mentally as she raged.

'It's all so damned transparent. They talk in terms of cost, but that's not the reality. It's cheaper to drag in this runt O'Hara — and I'm supposed to show him the ropes, take him in hand, train him, for God's sake! So he can make a decent showing at the interview and take the job away from me? What a nerve they've got! And when I've trained him, he'll sit in that damned interview in three months and will have just enough knowledge to put up a decent showing — and give the whole charade the appearance of being an open competition, open and above board. But that's not the end, is it?'

She turned, and stabbed a finger in Arnold's direction. 'All the while, you'll be sitting there smugly. I know what Powell Frinton has in mind when he talks about me acting as director but sharing responsibilities. He wants you to get a higher profile, at my expense. You — and they — know damned well I can do Brent-Ellis's job with one hand tied behind my back. But no, they'll give you some of the work to do, train you so that you also can undermine me in the interview.'

'I assure you, I've no desire—'

'Well, I'm not going to have it,' she hissed. 'I've worked hard for this chance, and I'm not going to have it all destroyed by a dirty-tricks campaign by you, or Powell Frinton — or Tom Patrick and the finance committee for that matter. I'll sort out that creepy bastard O'Hara. And you, Landon — you will not attend the interviews!'

'I've already said that I—'

'You heard me! You'll do what I say — do what you promised me. You'll tell Powell Frinton to his face that you've not the slightest intention of standing for this job. If you don't, believe me, I'll make your life hell — and I can do that, trust me!'

Anger began to course through Arnold's veins. He had no desire to apply for Brent-Ellis's job. He did not want to be shortlisted. He had been serious when he told Karen Stannard earlier that he was happy doing the job he currently held. But her attitude was annoying him. 'I don't take kindly to threats,' he said stiffly.

'Threats? You have no idea how I can make your life miserable! I'm telling you, Landon, step aside or else!'

Grimly, he shook his head. 'You're going about this the wrong way. If I step aside, it'll be because I think it's right to do so, not because you want me to.'

'If you step aside?' she yelped. 'Landon,' she warned, almost spitting out the words in unreasoning fury, 'you'll do as you're bloody well told!'

'No,' he snapped. 'I'll do what I want to do, and I'll do what I think is right.'

'You don't deserve the job — I do! I've worked for it. It's only right that it should be given to me.'

'I'll make my own decision about what's right, and what's wrong,' Arnold said in a cold voice.

There was a short silence. She stood there in front of him in a towering rage, spread-legged, shaking with anger, but it seemed only to enhance her beauty. Her eyes glowed, her whole body was alive with tension, and her sexuality had never been more apparent.

There was a tap on the door, and it opened slowly. Alan Farmer peered into the room. 'Karen,' he said a little nervously, 'if you don't mind, we need to leave. Our table . . .'

Karen Stannard did not even glance at him. She continued to glare at Arnold, but slowly her anger cooled as she regained control of herself. The message in her eyes was clear nevertheless. It boded ill for Arnold. Her voice was low and steady. 'Just two minutes, Alan, while I get my coat. Mr Landon and I . . . we're finished here.'

CHAPTER THREE

1

The delegates began to arrive in the early afternoon. Some were clearly taking the opportunity to use the conference as a chance to visit the North Country for leisure purposes. There was a programme outside the main conference for wives and partners and families — trips to Lindisfarne and Berwick, Edinburgh and the Borders. For many this would be the first time they had experienced the splendours of Northumberland: the long sweep of the beaches, the castles and tower houses, the majestic rise of the Cheviots in the hinterland. But most of the delegates would ignore the surrounding countryside — they would be immersed in the papers delivered on Triplism and Miniaturization, Style and Schematism in Celtic Iconography, Iron Age Bog Burials, and Human Sacrifice and Head Hunting.

The final meeting of the conference planning committee took place that afternoon, while the early delegates were being booked into their rooms in the country club. For the conference committee it was an opportunity to plug any gaps in the programme, finalize any small details that had gone wrong, confirm that everything was in order, with speakers properly sequenced, arrivals confirmed, distribution of learned papers properly organized.

'The final number of delegates is just short of two hundred,' Colin Norfolk announced. 'Not as good as last year, but creditable enough. And we have about sixty wives and partners, so I trust the social side of things will go well. Buses and all that suitably arranged . . .'

'It's all been checked,' Sheila Norfolk snapped irritably. Arnold had been a little surprised to see her at the committee meeting. She sat at the head of the table beside her husband, but there was an empty chair between them, as though symbolizing the fact of their marital differences. Arnold had heard the rumours that had been wide-ranging after Brent-Ellis's death: Colin Norfolk had been playing the field for years, and Sheila Norfolk's tumbling into bed with the Director of the Department of Museums and Antiquities had merely been her way of paying him back. It was just unfortunate that she had chosen the wrong moment to do it. But the events surrounding the last meeting, culminating in Brent-Ellis's death, had been sufficiently scandalous for Arnold to assume she would have kept her head down and absent herself from the conference. It wasn't the case. She had decided to brazen it out.

In a way he admired her for it. Colin Norfolk clearly was unhappy at her presence — his handsome features were marked with displeasure and he had lost his casual, flirtatious air — but she sat there as secretary with her chin up and her eyes challenging any who looked askance at her as the meeting opened. Arnold detected a certain embarrassment among the committee members, however, and it came to a head within minutes. Perhaps inevitably it came from the grim-visaged, balding Bernard Hewlett. There was clearly no love lost between him and the conference secretary.

'On a point of order, Chairman,' he rumbled menacingly. 'May I query the presence of Mrs Norfolk as secretary today at this meeting?'

There was a short, tense silence. 'That's not a point of order,' Sheila Norfolk said hotly, her deep-set eyes dark and glowering. 'I've every right to be here.'

'It's a matter for the chairman to decide,' Hewlett replied, without looking at her.

'It's nothing to do with the chairman. I've been secretary to this conference for three years.'

Hewlett raised his eyebrows, ignoring her. 'Chairman . . . ?' Colin Norfolk had paled. His narrow features were torn with doubt and anxiety. 'I'm not sure—'

'Then let me make it clear,' Hewlett interrupted coldly. 'I am surprised to see Mrs Norfolk here today. We are in the final stage of planning an important conference. We will be expecting delegates from all over the country. Eminent speakers have agreed to present papers. In the past we've gained a reputation for holding first-class, extremely important meetings that have had effects of significance on the archaeological world. But now . . . what do we have? At the penultimate meeting of this committee a disgraceful exhibition, licence, embarrassment of the kind that can only damage our reputation. The sad but scandalous death of one of our own members. And in view of the circumstances surrounding the demise of Mr Brent-Ellis, I am amazed that Mrs Norfolk has had the temerity to attend today. I cannot see that her presence here, and at the conference, can cause anything other than difficulty and embarrassment. I . . . I am overwhelmed by the fact she has not resigned.'

He sat back, his mouth set primly, his eyes firmly fixed on the chairman. Sheila Norfolk was rigid, waiting, but no one else spoke. At last, she said, 'I have no intention of resigning. The events you refer to . . . they are hardly unique. Certain men at these conferences have behaved in a similar manner. Indeed,' she added scornfully, glancing at her husband so that no one could have any doubt to whom she was referring, 'for some the conference appears to have been in the past only an opportunity to conduct liaisons . . . So, I see no reason for resignation. I've done all of the administrative work for this conference. I see no reason why I should now step aside.'

There was a long silence. Hewlett's mouth was grim as he glared around at the other committee members. 'I have stated *my* position,' he growled.

'Of course,' Sheila Norfolk said cuttingly as the silence was prolonged, 'it's open to the *committee* to ask for my resignation. And then appoint another person to handle the administration — at this late stage.'

There was a general uneasy shuffling in seats. No one dared to meet her glance and no one made any comment in the general discomfiture.

Sheila Norfolk turned to her persecutor. 'Mr Hewlett, perhaps *you'd* like to take on the responsibility for conference management?'

'Me?' His heavy eyelids flickered with alarm. 'That's out of the question. I've no time for such—'

'Drudgery?' she challenged him. 'I thought not.'

Nor was anyone else eager to take it on, Arnold noted.

They were a mixture of academics and professional archaeologists. Their work had been planning, discursive in nature, and now they were looking forward to a degree of junketing mingled with academic discussion. The last thing any of them would want was to be responsible for organizational matters they had not to date been involved in. So they remained silent, heads down. As Sheila Norfolk sat there, looking around the room, she was sticking it out defiantly. She was the conference secretary. She had a right to be there. And she knew no one would want to take over from her at this stage.

'So . . . shall we move on? Can we have a final run through of the papers?' Colin Norfolk suggested uneasily after the silence had lengthened, with Hewlett scowling at the ceiling, openly supported by none of his colleagues, and with one of them — Gareth Robbins — clearly enjoying his unease. The members agreed with the chairman in a relieved murmur and they spent the next half-hour checking that all was in order with speakers, supporting papers, and membership of evening discussion groups.

'There'll be no discussion group this evening, of course,' Norfolk announced, more at ease now, but pointedly ignoring his wife, 'because of the welcome reception, and then dinner afterwards. As usual, the first evening,' he explained for Arnold's benefit, 'is used as an opportunity for delegates to get to know each other, and to renew old acquaintances . . .'

Arnold caught the cynical glance Sheila Norfolk gave her estranged husband. He guessed that there would have been many occasions in the past when Colin Norfolk had 'renewed' old acquaintances — and made some new ones, as well. All, of course, female.

'As far as the dinner is concerned,' Gareth Robbins suggested, scratching his sandy hair, 'should we run through the seating arrangements, and the list of official guests? I see, for instance, that the list is rather larger than usual—'

'That's because of the involvement of the local authority, this year. Mr Landon, your department was invited to send in a list of appropriate people—'

'That's right. I'm sorry Miss Stannard isn't here for the committee meeting this afternoon,' Arnold replied, 'but she'll be arriving in time for the cocktail reception. It was she who finally produced the list of guests, after consultation with the authority. It reflects the departmental and local authority commitment to the conference, and also the fact that we are currently in the process of making a bid for Lottery cash to support an important archaeological dig in the area. She thought for that reason Mr Alan Farmer, who is helping finance the project, should be included, along with Councillor Patrick who is heading the submission committee, and Councillor Tremain, who is chairman of the finance committee—'

'It's a long list,' Robbins complained, and then shrugged. 'But I suppose—'

'We can't be churlish,' Sheila Norfolk snapped, 'when we've had so much administrative support from the authority. It's removed a large burden from my shoulders.'

'I thought it was the *secretary* who undertook all the burden of administration on her own shoulders,' Bernard Hewlett sneered, like a dog unwilling to relinquish a bone.

Colin Norfolk did not want to proceed down that track again. He looked at his notes, and then at her with anger in his eyes. She returned his glance coolly, almost challengingly, as though she no longer cared what he felt or did. 'I think we'll have to move on. It's far too late to have this kind of discussion,' he said in an irritated tone. 'The list is provided to us, at our invitation, and we cannot be seen to—'

Hewlett suddenly spoke again, still smarting from his earlier failure to remove Sheila Norfolk from the committee and the conference. 'There's one name at least on the list which I'd like to query.'

'And that is?'

'O'Hara. Steven O'Hara. Why is he to be an official guest?' There was a short silence. Colin Norfolk turned to Arnold.

'Can you help us on this?'

There was something in Colin Norfolk's expression that suggested he knew the reason behind Hewlett's objection. Arnold leaned forward. 'Mr O'Hara is the person who's been appointed to prepare the submission to the Lottery Heritage Commission. We're seeking support funding for the Stangrove Project,' Arnold explained.

'Is that good reason to invite him?' Hewlett demanded unpleasantly.

Colin Norfolk was uncertain whether he should allow the questioning to proceed. 'I'm not sure we should be second-guessing a guest list that's been prepared at Morpeth. I mean, we asked them to produce a list — it seems to me—'

'However it may seem to you, Chairman, *I* don't think Mr O'Hara is an appropriate person to be on the guest list,' Hewlett stated flatly. 'The man has a reputation.' He was clearly big on reputations, Arnold thought as Hewlett stared at him unwinkingly, almost as though this was all Arnold's fault. There was another short silence.

The chairman cleared his throat. 'I'm not sure . . . I don't feel—'

His wife interrupted, her voice sharp-edged as she stared at Hewlett, prepared to do battle with him on any ground.

'I'm fully aware of the reasons why Professor Hewlett might not wish to have Mr O'Hara as a guest at the conference. But the list was prepared by Morpeth, at our request. It's not for us to comment on the choice suggested. Nor is the conference to be regarded as a vehicle for the expression of Professor Hewlett's personal likes and dislikes.'

Hewlett's face slowly turned red. He glared his disapproval at Sheila Norfolk. 'I think it's very *much* our responsibility to comment, if people such as O'Hara are invited.'

'I repeat, this is not the place for personal arguments to be raised. Formally, we don't know what you're talking about, Professor Hewlett,' Sheila Norfolk said icily. Arnold felt she wanted to add it was not for the first time.

'I am talking about behaviour that is *unprofessional*,' Hewlett replied, in a sneering tone. There were undercurrents here, it was clear he was referring to her as much as to O'Hara. 'My dealings with O'Hara have led me to believe that the man is not a fit person to be seen in distinguished company of the kind we expect to appear at the SPA conference.'

'Not a fit person?' Sheila Norfolk queried, flushing, fully aware the attack was two-pronged. 'Do you wish to be more specific?'

Hewlett allowed a sly, superior smile to touch his lips. He settled back in his chair and folded his arms across his chest. 'It is not a matter I wish to discuss in public. But I have stated my views. It's for others to make decisions. Nevertheless, I have made my protest.'

'And is that formally to be *minuted*?' Sheila Norfolk asked coldly. 'That Mr Hewlett has an objection to someone on the guest list, but isn't prepared to substantiate it?'

Colin Norfolk shifted uneasily in his chair. He ran a despairing hand through his thick, swept-back hair. 'Now, come, come, we don't need to get too uptight about this. Professor Hewlett, you clearly feel . . . strongly about the presence of Mr O'Hara . . .' He hesitated, glanced around the group. 'And I think one or two of you know what Mr Hewlett bases his objections on. But this is all very . . . embarrassing . . .'

Sheila Norfolk turned her head slowly and stared at her husband. A malicious glint appeared in her eye. She would clearly be very happy at the thought of any form of embarrassment her husband might be subjected to, but she remained silent as he flushed, and continued. 'The fact is, O'Hara's name has been proposed for the guest list. The invitation has been issued. I don't see how we can change things at this late stage.'

'We should have seen the list before now,' Hewlett snapped.

'You *would* have seen it, if you'd been more involved, or given some assistance in the administration,' Sheila Norfolk countered. 'But then, *your* time is at a premium, isn't it, Professor Hewlett? Unlike the rest of us!'

'Please, I don't think we should squabble about this,' Norfolk pleaded desperately. 'It's all too late now, and in any case, the invitation is only for this evening. O'Hara won't be present for the conference as a whole—'

'He has in fact booked in for the first day also,' Sheila Norfolk corrected, 'not that you'd be aware of that.'

Colin Norfolk gave her a murderous glance.

'My point has been made, and my position is clear,' Hewlett said in a pompous tone.

Arnold was intrigued. He was aware that several heads around the table had nodded seriously when Hewlett had raised the issue. It was a matter clearly personal to Hewlett, and some of his cronies were aware of the problem, and agreed with him. But it was unlikely there would be any further enlightenment for the rest of the committee. He was to be left in the dark, and he could see that Colin Norfolk was eager to push on, and avoid any further embarrassment.

It was as well that Karen Stannard had not been there. She was no supporter of O'Hara and his name would probably have been added to her list under some sort of pressure, from Tom Patrick, perhaps. But she would have enjoyed the thought that the man she had not wanted to be appointed as consultant was not acceptable either, to some members of the conference committee, as an official guest of the Society of Professional Archaeologists.

As the meeting continued, Arnold felt it was likely to be a rather interesting dinner that evening, if Hewlett and his cronies made their views obvious to all. Karen Stannard would have enjoyed all this. Arnold was not inclined to fore-warn her.

2

The cocktail reception and conference dinner were tradition-
ally formal occasions and the male delegates were dressed in
dinner jackets, with the odd lounge suit appearing among
those who objected to formal wear. For some of the women,
of course, it had been an opportunity to raid their husband's
bank accounts for new dresses, and there was clearly a degree
of competition present, particularly among those spouses who
habitually attended the SPA conference as partners rather
than delegates. There was much air-kissing and handshak-
ing as delegates renewed old acquaintances and exchanged
personal gossip and archaeological anecdotes. The majority
of those present tended to be upwards of forty years of age.
There were a few small groups of young people, who were
dispersed about the room: research assistants, young lecturers, sons and daughters dragged along to the conference by
their parents.

When Karen Stannard entered the room there was an
audible murmur from the men who were stationed near the
door. Arnold smiled to himself. He might have guessed the
acting director of his department would outshine every other
woman in the room by dressing simply, but sensationally.
The dress was black, sheath-like and low-cut; her shoulders

were bare apart from a simple gold necklace and her hair was drawn back, exposing her throat and neck to perfection. She moved confidently, with a swaying motion that drew all male eyes, her hair glinted with colours of russet and gold, and her eyes were deep and dark, her mouth touched with a hint of amusement.

He was surprised when she walked directly across to him. 'Arnold,' she said in a soft, musical voice. 'Having a good time?'

'Not as much as you already are,' he smiled.

'The cynosure of all eyes.'

She was in a good mood. She smiled back, eyeing him with approval. 'You're very elegant yourself. I've not seen you in a dinner jacket before. Quite a different person . . . And you were here early, of course, because of the committee meeting. You gave my apologies?'

'Of course. May I get you a glass of wine?'

'There's one already here, Karen.' Alan Farmer was standing at her shoulder, holding out the glass he had brought, his eyes glazed with admiration as he stared at her.

'Alan! That's so kind of you. Have you been here long?'

He smiled diffidently. 'It's no great distance for me, from Stangrove. I . . . I rang your room a little while ago, but there was no answer.'

'Oh, I was probably in the shower,' she said, and Arnold noticed him shiver slightly at the image the remark presented him. Arnold also caught the mischievous glint in her eyes as she too noted the impact of her comment on Farmer, and was hard put to it not to smile. He felt he should move away. He suspected she was going to give Alan Farmer a hard, teasing time tonight and he didn't really want to be party to it. 'Would you excuse me, Miss Stannard, I think I ought to—'

'Before you go, Arnold,' she purred, detaining him with a hand on his arm, 'although this is not perhaps the time to talk business, I ought to tell you I had an excellent meeting with Councillor Tremain this afternoon, over finance. I managed to convince him—'

I bet you did, Arnold thought.

'—that the department shouldn't have to bear the full cost of Mr O'Hara's consultancy. And that I should have a new personal secretary. That will mean the additional burden of looking after Mr O'Hara won't be as heavy as I'd contemplated. And that, of course, also means that the chief executive's suggestion that you should take over part of the director's role won't be necessary.' There was a hint of triumph in her voice. 'I can undertake it all, with a personal assistant . . .'

'That's fine,' Arnold replied easily. 'It leaves me free to do what I enjoy doing best.'

There was a gleam of malice in her eyes. 'It will, of course, mean you won't obtain the *fullest* experience, before turning up for your interview . . .'

Arnold smiled. 'I agree. But there are experiences . . . and experiences. I'll have more time for fieldwork.'

As he moved away, he was absurdly pleased to see that her own smile had become a little disconcerted at his failure to rise to her bait, or acknowledge her minor triumph.

The room rapidly became crowded. He caught a glimpse of Paul Samuels and George Pym; Sue Lawrence was being somewhat monopolized in a corner by a young man with a red bow tie and a hovering manner, while Bernard Hewlett, flamboyant in a dark maroon dinner jacket and flowered waistcoat, was booming away at a coterie of respectful young delegates, probably about his latest thoughts on biomolecular palaeontology.

The official guests had arrived ahead of Karen Stannard — among them Councillor Tom Patrick and Councillor Tremain, who were being entertained by Colin Norfolk. The unconscious cause of the unpleasantness in the conference committee' Steven O'Hara, was standing near the drinks table, involved in deep discussion with Sheila Norfolk, and paying great attention to her considerable cleavage. She had taken trouble with her dress and from her gestures and body language, Arnold could see that she was out to impress there was no question of self-effacement after the Brent-Ellis incident. As she had done at the committee, she was intent on brazening it out at the dinner.

The noise levels were rising as the waitresses moved among the groups, replenishing the drinks of those who could not stagger as far as the drinks table, and the whole room was talking and not listening, laughing noisily at unfunny jokes, and generally demonstrating a determination to enjoy themselves.

The reception was being hosted by several publishers who specialized in academic books, mainly archaeology. They had been permitted by the conference committee to erect a stand at the back of the room to display a selection of their more recent texts — some of which had been commissioned from speakers at the conference itself. The publishers had not stinted themselves on the provision of refreshments. There were several good wines available, as well as the usual range of spirits and soft drinks. But then, the SPA conference was declared by all to be a prestigious event.

Arnold was looking over some of the new texts when he was joined by Gareth Robbins. 'This is always a prestigious event,' he announced, waving his glass of red wine.

'So I've been told, several times.'

'More than a few fakes among the gathering, of course, and a smattering of pseuds,' Robbins grinned vaguely at Arnold. 'But then, you can expect that, can't you? After all, that's where the money largely comes from — the wannabes, who can't make it but think that if they come to conferences, rub shoulders with the great and the good, and generally toady up to people like old Hewlett there, that's all it takes to make their careers!' He hiccupped. 'That, and a concentration on the indigestible, learned papers that get served up to them.'

'So why do *you* come?'

'To get pissed. And once in a while, to get laid.' He leered at Arnold, already more than a little inebriated. 'I listen to the conference papers, of course, the ones that interest me . . . but body and soul can take only so much of that sort of thing, don't you know?' His eyes were somewhat glazed as they searched the room. 'I see our estimable chairman is looking after the top table guests. And Sheila's there, hovering at the fringes, exposing her bosom to that fellow O'Hara. Not bad, not bad at all for her age. She's not unshaggable, you know . . . but then, your colleague Brent-Ellis found that out, didn't he?'

Arnold was disinclined to talk or think about Simon Brent-Ellis. 'She can be a pretty formidable lady.'

'Looks like O'Hara may well find that out for himself before the night is out. The way she's wiggling her hips at him he could be in for a good time. But she certainly gave old Hewlett as good as she got this afternoon, didn't she?' Robbins leaned forward confidentially towards Arnold. 'You know, I have a theory about that pompous bastard. I suspect he lusts after Sheila Norfolk himself, has done for years, but was never man enough even to put it in her hand, so to speak. And then she goes and does it at long last with Brent-Ellis, of all people, for God's sake! But then, that wasn't really desperation on her part — she just wanted to show up dear Colin, that's all. And Brent-Ellis was available. But I'll tell you this' — he winked owlishly 'if she hadn't been caught, you know, I reckon she'd have *told* hubby all about it anyway. After the event. Not that he didn't deserve to be cuckolded. See that woman over there? Norfolk laid her last year.' He waved his glass vaguely in the direction of the crowd. 'And that nubile blonde there . . . he stuffed her the year before . . .' He cackled to himself. 'Perquisites of office. Maybe I should try for conference committee chairman . . .'

Arnold was still watching O'Hara and Sheila Norfolk. The Irishman certainly seemed to be enjoying himself. She was smiling coquettishly, the fingers of one hand resting lightly on his arm, and it was clear he thought he had made a conquest, leaning confidentially across her, whispering in her ear and being rewarded by a burst of laughter, and a playful, incongruously girlish, slap. Arnold caught the irritated glances that her husband sent in her direction from time to time, as she laughed and flirted with O'Hara. At Arnold's elbow, Gareth Robbins belched, and he caught the gust of stale wine in his nostrils.

'She's doing it to annoy her husband, of course,' Robbins leered, 'but why pick O'Hara? I'd have been prepared to accommodate her over the weekend. Though I suppose she'd pick that little bastard just to make things worse — I mean, Brent-Ellis was in the *most annoying* category, because Colin Norfolk couldn't stand him, so I guess that's why she laid him. As for O'Hara, he's disliked by most of those who've come into contact with him, and after Hewlett's performance in the committee she'd be getting at him as well as her husband by laying O'Hara tonight.'

Arnold was curious. 'I don't really know O'Hara — just spent a day with him, really, over the consultancy contract. But what's the problem people seem to have with him? I mean, you say everyone who knows him dislikes him; Hewlett clearly has a view of him; I gathered, when I was up at the Stangrove dig, that Paul Samuels and he have a problem . . .'

'Ah, well, that's really where it all starts,' Robbins murmured confidentially, half closing one eye in a knowing manner. 'Samuels was doing some research under the supervision of Professor Hewlett. He was interviewed at one point by O'Hara — he was working at one of the York newspapers then and had been writing an article on Roman York. Anyway, somehow or other O'Hara got wind of the details of Samuels's research. Samuels was expecting to publish his findings at the end of the year. But O'Hara jumped the gun, sensationalized the material Samuels was working on, even sold a script on it to a TV company, apparently, and Paul Samuels was jumping up and down about it. He was furious both with O'Hara and Hewlett.'

'Where does Bernard Hewlett come into it?'

'Ah, well, Bernard, dear chap, was acting as supervisor to Samuels — he was head of the department and as all those old buffers do, they supervise, do no bloody work on the research, but then claim equal billing when the credits start to roll. So he was a bit pissed off as well, but it then got worse when Samuels accused Hewlett of leaking the details of the research to O'Hara. That sent Hewlett off like a sky rocket — he had a public argument with Samuels and later with O'Hara — but the bloody Irishman cheerfully told them both to sod off, and went his own way. He'd sold the script so why should he care? It's still rumbling on, though, the quarrel . . . there's lawyers, and injunctions and all sorts out there, and no one is very happy with the guy at the centre of it all — our little friend O'Hara.'

Not that it seemed to bother the Irishman. He was in the centre of an organization which was the kind that would always feed on gossip, he had at least two of his enemies in the room — though Arnold also recalled the way in which Sue Lawrence had greeted his appearance at the Stangrove dig — but he was quite unabashed. He was clearly enjoying his *tête à tête* with Sheila Norfolk. He had his arm around her waist now as he swigged at his whisky, and she was leaning into him provocatively, her bosom crushed against his chest as the noise and the laughter swirled around them. Committed to the entertainment of the small group of official guests, Colin Norfolk glowered in displeasure at a distance, until there was an announcement at the doorway that dinner was now being served. Then he broke away and moved purposefully across the room to speak to both O'Hara and Sheila Norfolk. O'Hara grinned at him and said something which caused Colin Norfolk to stiffen, and respond angrily, before steering his wife away. She was giggling, and cast an amused glance back over her shoulder in O'Hara's direction, while Norfolk gripped her elbow, pushing her towards the official guests and muttering fiercely in her unheeding ear. It was clear trouble was in the air, Arnold thought, before he lost sight of them in the crowd.

There was a general milling of bodies outside the door as delegates jostled to check the notice board for the seating plan. Gradually the crowd thinned, and when Arnold made his way to the board, just behind Gareth Robbins, he noted that George Pym had rescued Sue Lawrence from her bow-tied admirer, and was leading her in to dinner. 'I think you can follow us, Arnold — you're on the same table as us,' Pym said. 'The Stangrove group, you might say: Sue and me and Paul, Miss Stannard and you, and Alan Farmer.'

'I thought Mr Farmer was to be one of the official guests.'

George Pym winked. 'He was — and was located on the top table. O'Hara was to be with us. But I suspect a deal has been done because Farmer preferred to be seated at our table.' He grinned knowingly at Arnold. 'I wonder why?'

The table for the official guests was at the far end of the dining room, but the circular table on which Arnold found himself was not too far away. He took his place between Alan Farmer and Paul Samuels, facing Karen Stannard, on Farmer's left, George Pym and Sue Lawrence. They quickly agreed on a choice of wine, ordered by Farmer, and settled down to dinner, which was quickly served. Arnold found himself isolated to a certain extent as far as conversation was concerned. Farmer concentrated on Karen Stannard, George Pym on Sue Lawrence, while Paul Samuels seemed withdrawn and disgruntled. His eyes rarely strayed from the scene at the top table. 'Look at him,' he muttered. 'Behaving like the pig he is.'

Arnold had no doubt as to whom he was referring. O'Hara was ensconced beside Sheila Norfolk, and the animated conversation they had been having earlier was continuing. As he watched, Arnold saw Colin Norfolk, red-faced, rise to his feet and step behind his wife, say something to her. She shook her head, shrugged, and then gestured in the direction of Arnold's table. Colin Norfolk glared, then snapped something at his wife before returning to his own seat.

'He's bloody gate-crashed, it looks like,' Paul Samuels grumbled. 'And got away with it, too.'

Alan Farmer glanced to the top table and smiled edgily. 'I'm afraid that was my doing. I spoke to him earlier — suggested he might care to change places with me. I hate top tables. He seems to be otherwise inclined.'

'Crawling bastard,' Samuels muttered angrily, and took a long draught of wine.

'I'll drink to that,' George Pym added, surprisingly, glowering in O'Hara's direction. Sue Lawrence flushed and put a hand on his muscular arm. She caught Arnold's glance. There was a vague uncertainty in her eyes and she seemed confused. She leaned towards George and spoke to him in a low voice, almost admonishingly.

The evening progressed pleasantly enough for Arnold. Paul Samuels had little to say, and got steadily more inebriated as time passed, George and Sue Lawrence talked a little about the dig with him, but most of the time he was entertained by the manner in which Karen Stannard dangled Alan Farmer on a teasing string. He was clearly infatuated by her, and she was enjoying her little triumph. In a sense it was unlike her, for although she used her sexuality like an offensive weapon on occasions, in order to achieve her own ends, this was the first time he had seen her use it casually, for mere entertainment purposes. Once or twice she glanced in his direction, as though checking to see whether he was aware of her triumph. He felt a little sorry for Alan Farmer. He suspected the man would be doomed to disappointment, if he was taking the flirtation seriously. There was no doubt he was overwhelmed — but Arnold had to agree that she looked absolutely stunning in her black sheath dress.

At the conclusion of the dinner they were advised that drinks were still available in the room where the reception had been held, and there was a general scraping of chairs for the exodus back to the place where they had all started. As the people seated at the top table began to move, Steve O'Hara buttonholed Councillor Patrick for a moment, until Sheila Norfolk came up and took him by the hand, drawing him away. Tom Patrick looked displeased about something, but Colin Norfolk's brow was thunderous.

Arnold moved back to the reception room with the others. He had no intention of staying long, and he noted that the two councillors, Patrick and Tremain, soon made their apologies to Colin Norfolk and left, though separately. There was no sign of Paul Samuels and a little while after Sue Lawrence excused herself, George Pym also left the room. Alan Farmer made his way through the thinning throng and joined Arnold, holding a glass of red wine. 'Well, I must say, it's been a pleasant occasion, Landon. Is this a regular occurrence for you?'

Arnold shook his head. 'No, it's the first time I've attended an SPA conference. It's rather . . . more uninhibited than I expected.'

Farmer laughed and looked around the room. 'Yes . . . one has a predetermined view of archaeologists, expecting them to be dry as dust, and circumspect in their behaviour. But some seem to be letting their hair down.' His glance fixed on Sheila Norfolk as he spoke. She was draping her arm across O'Hara's shoulder and laughing up at him provocatively. Farmer turned back to Arnold, his tone suddenly serious. 'Karen was telling me earlier that you and she are to be interviewed for the post vacated by Brent-Ellis's death.' He hesitated, but when Arnold made no reply, he went on, 'And she tells me that fellow O'Hara is also involved as a candidate. He's hardly qualified, is he? I mean, he's little experience, from what I can gather. How on earth did he get shortlisted?'

Arnold shrugged. Idly, he was watching O'Hara as the man took Sheila Norfolk by the elbow and began to manoeuvre her towards the door, handing his glass to a waiter and taking hers from her, draining it and setting it down on a table. Arnold was aware of Colin Norfolk, also watching them as they moved among the others in the room. Then all three were lost to sight, and Arnold turned back to Alan Farmer.

'I gather from Karen that O'Hara's generally disliked in the archaeological world,' Farmer was continuing. 'It wouldn't be a good idea if he got the departmental job — and I know a little about him, too . . . Perhaps if I were to put in a word at the right place, have a chat with Tom Patrick, maybe . . .'

'How have you come across O'Hara?' Arnold asked curiously. 'Apart from our meeting the other day, that is.'

Farmer sipped his wine, and grimaced. 'We were involved in this plagiarism thing.'

'We?'

'Oh, sorry, I mean the television production company I'm involved with. You probably heard us mention it the other day. The matter had come up before I joined the board, but I've seen it in the minutes. O'Hara contracted to develop this programme on Roman York — you know, there's a lot of interest in archaeology and history programmes at the moment — then there was a lot of noise from Paul Samuels and others about plagiarism, and the company got an injunction slapped on it . . . it's all been very unpleasant. I don't blame Samuels in any way, but this O'Hara character . . . not the kind of man who'd fit in well at the Department of Museums and Antiquities, I'd say . . .' He was silent for a little while, observing the chattering crowd with narrowed eyes. 'Karen Stannard would make a good director, in my view . . .' He glanced at Arnold, somewhat sheepishly. 'But then, I'm biased. I've spent rather a lot of time with her recently, discussing the Stangrove dig . . . And I'm rather taken with her, really.'

He glanced around and his features brightened. She was making her way towards them at that moment.

'Alan,' she murmured. 'Sorry to keep you waiting. Would you mind very much, getting another drink for me? Since I'm staying for the conference, and not driving back tonight, I can let my hair down.'

As he bustled away, she smiled at Arnold and gestured towards the door. 'I see another little scandal starting. I just passed them as they were heading out towards the terrace.'

'Who?'

'Didn't you see?' She shook her head, smiling contemptuously. 'The way things are going, O'Hara's going to make a fool of himself with Sheila Norfolk. She really is a predator, that woman.'

When Alan Farmer returned, Arnold excused himself and edged away. There was more than one bird of prey in the room. And whatever might be going on between O'Hara and Sheila Norfolk, Arnold had no desire to watch while Karen Stannard made a fool of Alan Farmer.

3

The full business of the conference started properly next day, and a succession of learned and expert speakers ascended the stage to deliver their papers. While spouses, partners and family members set off on a trip to Berwick, those official guests who had stayed overnight took their leave and the hotel staff moved in to clear their rooms. In the main conference hall, meanwhile, the delegates declared themselves entranced by, and supported with thunderous acclamation, presentations on Roman Quarries at Gebel Dokan, Furnaces and Hypocausts at Vindolanda, and the Role of Ritual Vessels in Celtic Liturgy. The discussion groups that evening were intense in their enthusiasm, and erudite conversations continued in the bar until the early hours of the morning. The observant noted that some of the unattached delegates had begun to pair off late in the day, ostensibly to carry on learned discussion, but the cynical at the conference suggested that more carnal matters were probably foremost in their minds.

The following morning there was an excursion to the Roman Wall for the hangers-on while a professor from Denmark explained in a thick accent the archaeological conclusions he had drawn from a chariot burial at La

Gorge-Meillet in north-west France. Exuberant sessions on Animism and Zoomorphic Monsters, Symbolism and Imagery, Miniaturization, and Micropalaeontology followed. The last was somewhat marred by the performance of Bernard Hewlett who — clearly in a bad temper about something — created an unprecedented disturbance when from the floor he started an argument with the distinguished presenter on the stage. It began in a civilized enough manner but when the presenter continued to disagree with Hewlett the discussion became angry, heated, and abusive. The evening discussion sessions were also diverted by a snappish confrontation between the chairman and secretary of the conference. The Norfolks were clearly not seeing eye to eye, and it was obvious that the discussion, though purporting to be academic, had undertones of marital fury.

All was much calmer on the third day of the conference, as was fitting for its conclusion. There was some evidence of boredom as delegates began to drift away in the early afternoon, making the transparent excuse that they had a long way to drive, but the presentations on Ambiguity and Obscurity in Cult Expression, and Skeuomorphic Decoration of Iron Age Axe-shafts, did retain the interest of the more dogged among the enthusiasts. Colin Norfolk's closing conference address was delivered to a half-empty auditorium.

Rooms were cleared, baggage packed, farewells taken, bills for extras paid. The cars left one by one, and the small army of cleaners descended on the rooms to prepare everything for the next inhabitants of the country club. They began to arrive that evening: a golfing convention from the Midlands, armed with clubs, a determination to enjoy themselves, and an optimistic conviction that this year they would achieve far better cards than they had previously managed. All would be proven the following day.

It began to rain at three in the morning. It was a heavy downpour, hammering on the roof of the country club, driving hard against the long glass windows of the lounge overlooking the practice green. The rain was accompanied by violent claps of thunder, and jagged flashes of lightning. The clouds remained heavy and thunderous at dawn and what Colonel Arkwright, chairman of the club, described as a regular monsoon — bad as anything I saw in India', saturated the golf course attached to the country club. The secretary to the convention was forced to make an announcement at breakfast to the assembled members that it was sad, but clear, that for that day play was impossible. The members of the convention were displeased, but assuaged their sorrows by sitting in the lounge, watching the rain, playing Scrabble or bridge, discussing golf and maintaining a steady flow of alcohol between bar and tables. All agreed, however, that the day was a washout.

The following morning remained grey and the course was waterlogged so general play was still impossible. A few hardy souls trooped out to walk part of the course, commenting upon their misfortunes. One man walked alone. Major Tremble had come out suitably garbed against the inclement weather: flat cap, Barbour jacket, cavalry twill trousers protected by heavy boots. He had brought a putter with him, and he swished it in disappointed swings from side to side as he walked, sending up a spray to either side. He had thought retirement would be better than this, and cursed the Northumberland weather.

It was on the return walk that he spotted what appeared to be a bundle of clothing in the gorse bushes. At first he thought it was a pile of rubbish that had been blown along from the hotel area by the storm. It was only some fifty yards from the terrace at the side of the country club. But its size and bulk reminded him of other sights he had seen, in Africa, in the Gulf, and in Northern Ireland. Grimly, he stepped away from the path and headed towards the screening gorse bushes.

When he stood over his discovery his hands were cold and in spite of himself, he shivered slightly. He hadn't expected to find this sort of thing on a golfing convention. And something — probably foxes — had already been gnawing at the thing that lay at his feet.

Before turning away to hurry back to the hotel, and the telephone, he leaned forward, inspecting the damage done by the foxes. The face had been badly torn, but he could see that the body was that of a man, sprawled on its side, one arm folded underneath the body, the other outflung with fingers curled. The heavy rain had not entirely obliterated the scuff marks in the grass, scored by dragging heels. The major guessed the body had been dragged from some other location, before being dumped among the gorse. It was also possible it had been further moved into the open from the protection of the gorse by wildlife.

The major explained his find to the hotel manager, giving his views as to what he believed to have happened. Then he told the conference secretary, who was much disturbed. It was obvious that this would have an effect upon the success of the golfing competition.

The hotel manager checked out the major's story and then returned to the hotel. He was grim of face as he telephoned the police. This publicity would do the hotel no good at all. But he was able to confirm what Major Tremble had said.

The person out there near the gorse bushes was dressed in a dinner jacket, had red hair, and was very dead.

CHAPTER FOUR

1

Detective Chief Inspector Culpeper scowled at Detective
Inspector Farnsby. 'Two *hundred*?'

'I'm afraid so, sir . . . It was an international conference,
and there were delegates from all over. About sixty or so from
the south, thirty from the Midlands . . .' He consulted his
list. 'Then there were some fifteen from Wales, twenty from
overseas — Denmark, France, Germany, and the rest from
the northern counties.'

Culpeper expelled his breath slowly. 'That's bloody
impossible!'

'That's the way it is, sir.'

The resignation in Farnsby's voice irritated Culpeper.
He gathered up the papers on his desk and nodded towards
the door. 'Come on, we'd better get along to the Chief
Constable. He wants to talk to us about this. But it's obvious the thing is going to be more than we can handle. Two
hundred, scattered all over the place . . .'

He marched down the corridor, a burly, thick-waisted,
middle-aged man who was looking forward to retirement
and a hassle-free last couple of years. It was all very well
for Farnsby, young, fast-track graduate, keen and looking
to the heights, but this kind of investigation was the last

thing Culpeper wanted. He had leave coming up soon, his wife Margaret had booked a caravan site in Normandy, and although Culpeper was not particularly keen on travelling abroad — he much preferred Seahouses, the Ship Inn, boat trips out to the Farne Islands and fishing off the Coquet —at least it would mean he'd be difficult to contact, in an emergency. That was Margaret's theory, although having been a copper's wife for thirty years and more she should know better.

And now they had a murder on their hands where the possible witnesses — perhaps including the killer himself numbered two hundred, and had been dispersed to the four winds.

The Chief Constable gestured to them to take seats in front of his desk. He himself rose to his feet and stood with his back to the window, leaning against the radiator. He preferred to look down on his colleagues when they visited his office. Culpeper wondered about the psychological implications of that, from time to time. It was a practice among small men, he understood, but the chief was tall, and his ego oversized. Maybe his soul was small.

A big, hulking, heavy-jowled man, the Chief Constable nevertheless showed a precision in his dress that was rumoured to impress the ladies, as did his quick, dark eyes, and the elegant frosting of his hair at the temples. He was well regarded among the county set, Culpeper had heard, and led an impressive social life, in both hunting and masonic circles. Dinner parties with the Lord Lieutenant were his scene. It was perhaps why he tended to regard Culpeper with a certain amount of disdain: a Durham pit village background, and a slow haul up from local bobby on the beat was not the kind of experience that was familiar to him. He'd never had to pick up the remains of decapitated suicides on the rail tracks from the pitheads. Neither had Farnsby. Now, the Chief Constable folded his arms, and gazed solemnly at the two men in front of him. His tone was deep, and carefully modulated. 'So what do we know about this man?'

Culpeper consulted his notes. 'Preliminary enquiries tell us his name was Steven O'Hara. Somewhat chequered background, trained as an accountant, worked in that capacity for a while, then turned to journalism—'

'So the papers will have a high time of it,' the Chief Constable sneered.

'—but currently working as a consultant for the local authority at Morpeth. He was a guest at a dinner at the country club, where he was found murdered—'

'No doubt about that?'

'Murder?' Culpeper blinked. 'No, sir. Heavy blow to the back of the head. When we conducted a search we found a tyre iron near the terrace, thrown among the bushes. We think it's the murder weapon. No great attempt to hide it, panicked, maybe. Forensic are working on it. But whether we'll get much from it, after those weather conditions—'

'What about the man who found him?' the Chief Constable interrupted.

'Interviewed but ruled out of our enquiries,' Culpeper replied in clipped tones. 'A retired army major, golf-mad, would have arrived at the hotel only after the murder was committed. We calculate the body had been lying out on the golf course for four days, sir.'

The Chief Constable clucked his tongue impatiently. '*Modus operandi*?'

Culpeper glanced at Farnsby. The younger man cleared his throat self-consciously. 'I've had an inch-by-inch, finger-tip inspection of the site organized, sir. I've also spoken to forensic for their preliminary thoughts and interviewed some of the local people who were at the conference. It looks to us as though O'Hara met someone on the terrace at the side of the hotel. There are no particular signs of a struggle — there's been heavy rain recently and that's made things more difficult — but the general view we've reached is that O'Hara was struck down there, and then dragged off to the bushes on the golf course. For concealment.'

'When?'

'He was wearing a dinner jacket, sir. So, obviously, it would have happened on the first night of the SPA conference.'

'Witnesses?'

Farnsby shook his head. 'None have come forward to date, sir. So it's going to mean taking statements, reconstructing O'Hara's movements the night he died—'

'Which is something we can't handle on our own,' Culpeper interrupted.

The Chief Constable's chin came up questioningly, his eyes were cold as he stared at Culpeper. He did not like his DCI and had made that clear on a number of occasions. He regarded him as over the hill, a man too concerned with taking an easy ride towards retirement, and someone with a chip on his shoulder because he felt he had been overlooked and undervalued in his career. Farnsby was more to his taste, as an eager, thrusting young officer with the right kind of background. 'Just what exactly do you mean by that, Culpeper?'

Culpeper thrust out a dogged chin to match the Chief Constable's own. 'O'Hara attended a conference, sir. He was a guest at the opening dinner. He was killed that night. His body wasn't found immediately, there was a lapse of four days. In that time the people who were at the conference — who would be able to help us in our enquiries — have been scattered all over the place. This is a big job, sir, with our manpower there's no way we can handle it. The killer could be anyone of more than two hundred people who were around at that time—'

'There'll be a large number, surely, who you can eliminate quickly,' the Chief Constable demurred.

'Only after we've interviewed them, sir. I repeat, it's a big job. We'll need assistance.'

He knew the Chief Constable would not like what he was hearing, nor its implications. He was a man jealous of his own patch.

'This is *our* murder, Culpeper,' the Chief Constable growled. 'I'm not happy at the thought of handing over to other forces—'

'We've no choice,' Culpeper insisted. 'We'll have to call for help — from the Midlands, from Wales, from the Met and we'd better run a check through Interpol also, in respect of the delegates from overseas. The only alternative is to tie up a large number of officers in our own force — and I hardly think you'll be agreeable to that. Sir.'

The Chief Constable's eyes gleamed, he was not happy with Culpeper's tone. Sarcastically, he enquired, 'So what advice would you be offering me, Culpeper?'

Stubbornly, Culpeper ignored the tone of voice. 'We must get in touch with the other forces, and ask for assistance. Someone here will have to be in charge of liaison, of course; local enquiries can be mounted speedily, but contacting the delegates who are scattered around the country will require close control. I would suggest that Farnsby can get on the job questioning the local contacts, seek for witnesses; I could undertake the liaison duties, link up with the other forces through our central headquarters unit, and coordinate the information as it comes in. To support that, I'll need—'

'No,' the Chief Constable almost purred. 'I don't think that's the best way forward. In the circumstances I have something else in mind.' He fixed Culpeper with a malicious glare. 'You're always telling us how you've come up through the ranks, a long, hard slog, Culpeper. You claim to have local contacts and knowledge *par excellence* — in a manner that Farnsby, and I for that matter, do not. So I don't think it's the sensible way forward for Farnsby to undertake that task. It's more up your street, wouldn't you agree?'

Culpeper scowled. The Chief Constable was justified in one respect: Culpeper was aware he had boasted often enough of his own skills and local knowledge, the kind of understanding of the North East and its communities that in his view Farnsby, for all his schooling, could never achieve. He shrugged. 'It's just a matter of the best use of manpower. I *could* undertake the local checks but my time would necessarily be limited, and it would interfere with my control of liaison—'

'But that's the point,' the Chief Constable interrupted softly. 'We could put someone else in as control. Detective Inspector Farnsby.'

Culpeper sat up straighter in his seat. He glanced at Farnsby. The man's saturnine features betrayed alarm momentarily, and then settled back into their customary impassivity. 'But control . . . liaison . . . that should be done by a senior officer—'

'Farnsby is senior enough,' the Chief Constable suggested, with a hint of malicious triumph in his tone. 'And it will give him the opportunity to develop his skills, liaising with senior officers from other forces. Naturally, you are the *senior* officer, Culpeper, but your role is an important one — using your local knowledge. The fact that you'll report to Farnsby, for liaison purposes . . . that's merely a matter of form. You'll still be in nominal charge, of course. But what we want is the most efficient use of our resources, and a swift end to our investigation. This seems to me the best way forward. Don't you agree, Chief Inspector?'

Farnsby sat very still, stiff-legged. Culpeper's features began to turn purple. 'I would wish to register a formal complaint about this, if the decision is taken.'

'It's taken, Culpeper,' the Chief Constable said dismissively, 'and your complaint is noted. Now perhaps you two can get down to details, and let me have a report in due course . . .'

* * *

Culpeper was still in a foul mood when he visited the premises of the local authority at Morpeth the following day. He felt that Farnsby had let him down, in not adding his own protest to the Chief Constable's decision. Farnsby had argued he was in no position to dispute the decision and to a certain extent the arrangement made sense. But Culpeper did not see it that way, and neither would the senior officers in the other forces. In their eyes, Culpeper would be seen to have been passed over, in favour of a younger, less senior man.

The Chief Constable had always shown signs of favour towards Farnsby — admired his keenness, his background, recognized his potential. Culpeper he saw as a man of dinosaurian tendencies, one who dwelled in the past, an old-style copper stuck in a rut of his own dogged digging. And to a certain extent, grudgingly, Culpeper was forced in moments of self-analysis to admit there was some justification for the view. But it was another matter to hand over control of the enquiry to an officer junior to Culpeper, and fob the DCI off with the local enquiries.

It was a nudge of course, a not so gentle push towards the oblivion of retirement.

So he was not in the best of moods when he entered the office of the local authority's chief executive, Mr Powell Frinton. The lean, grim-faced lawyer came forward to shake his hand and introduce him to the other man already in the room. 'This is Councillor Patrick. I thought it would be useful if he were in attendance, since it was Mr Patrick who was involved in the consultancy appointment of Mr O'Hara.' He sniffed, as though he had caught the whiff of an unpleasant odour under his pinched nostrils. 'A bad business, certainly, a bad business.'

Culpeper shook hands with the tall, sharp-eyed man facing him. He had never met Patrick before but he had heard of him. The man's campaign for office had been well reported in the newspapers since he had used as his main platform the promise to eliminate corruption in the council. He was reckoned to be a successful businessman, owner of one of the largest training agencies in the north. Maybe he'd got tired of business and thought local politics would give him new satisfactions — and in due course, honours, of course. Culpeper was cynical enough to believe few people entered public service for altruistic reasons.

Culpeper took a seat at the boardroom table and placed his notebook ostentatiously in front of him. 'So, Mr O'Hara was appointed as a consultant by the authority.'

'That's right,' Powell Frinton replied. 'But perhaps Mr Patrick can explain the relevant details.'

Culpeper took notes as Patrick spoke of the Stangrove Project, the problems of funding it from local authority coffers, the decision that had been taken to make a bid for Lottery funding to support the dig, and his committee's appointment of Steven O'Hara.

Culpeper frowned. 'Why did you think it necessary to appoint an outsider? You have personnel in your own department . . . Museums and Antiquities? Why didn't you use those?'

Tom Patrick shrugged. 'The committee felt that particular skills were required, skills in short supply within the authority.'

Culpeper caught a slight movement of Powell Frinton's narrow head. 'So you wanted someone with a journalistic background?'

Patrick hesitated. His brow was furrowed seriously. 'Not necessarily . . . but it was thought to be useful. A facility with words . . . and numbers — Mr O'Hara had an accounting background as well.'

'Mr O'Hara had not in fact undertaken the writing of such submissions previously,' Powell Frinton said, flagging a certain disapproval by his manner, 'but I have to say that after his appointment the committee was very impressed by his preliminary submission. It required but little change — so the journalistic background proved to be useful.'

Culpeper nodded. 'I see . . . So you advertised for a consultant, and O'Hara applied.' There was a short silence. Culpeper looked up. 'Didn't you?'

Powell Frinton pinched his nostrils between finger and thumb. 'Not exactly. We . . . Mr O'Hara was *recommended* to us.'

'By whom?'

Tom Patrick shrugged. He suddenly seemed a little uneasy. He drew his heavy eyebrows together and inspected his elegant cuffs. 'The recommendation . . . it wasn't quite like that. It was on the grapevine, really. It was discussed in committee. I can't quite remember who came up with the name . . .'

Powell Frinton cleared his throat in a way that reinforced the disapproval Culpeper had sensed earlier. 'We were keen to get the matter resolved quickly. We were under financial constraints; O'Hara's background seemed a useful one . . . and we wanted to get the submission completed within a specified time limit. So, perhaps . . . the committee cut a few corners.'

A practice that would have been anathema to the narrow-minded, regulation-driven chief executive, Culpeper considered. 'So you took him on, without knowing much about his background, then?'

'He was interviewed,' Powell Frinton replied stiffly. 'With others. He seemed the most appropriate appointment.'

Culpeper sighed, making clear his doubts about the manner in which the authority had organized things. 'All right, so you take this man on with a consultancy contract, he produces a draft submission, and then you all go off to this archaeological conference . . .'

'Not quite so,' Powell Frinton said quickly. '*I* was not present. Councillors Tremain and Patrick were the representatives of the authority on that occasion. Along with members of the relevant department, and O'Hara, of course.'

'I see. Did *you* stay there overnight, Mr Patrick?'

Tom Patrick shook his head, frowning. 'No. Joe Tremain and I, we both left shortly after dinner.'

'Together?'

'We left the hotel together, but in separate cars. Joe was heading north to Berwick, I believe — I was coming back to Morpeth. So we travelled separately.'

'Had you been drinking, sir?' Culpeper asked.

'Not a great deal,' Patrick replied, with a slight smile. 'It's possible I was over the limit, but I wasn't stopped at all, so . . .'

'So it's all a bit late, now,' Culpeper agreed. 'Did you see O'Hara when you left?'

'No. He was still inside, I believe. I think . . .' Patrick hesitated, and glanced uncertainly at the chief executive. 'I got the impression he was with a lady . . . in the area used for the reception. I couldn't see who she was. There was a bar there.'

Culpeper nodded. It was something to look into. He stared at Patrick, and then at Powell Frinton. 'I think I'd like to see the papers relevant to his appointment . . . it'll help on background. Otherwise, maybe that'll do for now. Unless there's anything else you want to add, gentlemen?'

There was a short silence. The two men glanced at each other. Then Powell Frinton laced his fingers together primly. 'There is one other thing, though it may not be relevant. The committee — they were very happy with Mr O'Hara's preliminary report, as I intimated. Apart from some minor amendments — at Miss Stannard's prompting — it seemed a good piece of work.'

Tom Patrick shifted uneasily in his seat. Culpeper frowned, struck by a sudden thought. 'Who would have done the report if you hadn't called for an outside consultant?'

'Miss Stannard was working on it,' Powell Frinton replied, after a slight hesitation.

'Where's the report now?'

Powell Frinton inspected his fingers carefully. 'It's in the hands of Mr Landon. Miss Stannard . . . well, she hasn't time to deal with it now, because of her assumption of other duties. You'll have heard of the . . . the unfortunate demise of Mr Brent-Ellis.' When Culpeper nodded, the chief executive added, 'She has taken over his duties.'

'So if I want to see the report, I can talk to Landon?'

'Assuredly.' Powell Frinton wriggled, uncharacteristically uneasy for a man who was normally in cold control of himself. 'But this brings us to the issue which . . . which I think I should mention to you.'

'Issue?' Culpeper asked, suddenly interested in the tension that seemed to have arisen in the room.

'The death of Mr Brent-Ellis.' Powell Frinton set his mouth primly, thinking for a few moments before choosing his words with care. 'The vacancy caused as a result of Mr Brent-Ellis's demise has to be filled. In the short term, it was decided that Miss Stannard should be asked to . . . as they say . . . hold the fort. But interviews were then to be held for the position to be filled permanently.'

'What's this got to do with O'Hara?'

Powell Frinton took a deep breath. For some reason he was unable to meet Culpeper's glance. 'Before his death, Mr O'Hara was informed that he had been shortlisted as a candidate for the post of director of the department.'

* * *

Arnold had been attending a departmental meeting where Karen Stannard had been outlining some changes of responsibility that she wanted implemented immediately. She had taken the opportunity to move into Simon Brent-Ellis's room as early as possible, and she had also moved the former director's secretary to a more distant location, declaring she would require Miss Sansom's office for her new personal assistant when appointed. The dragon qualities of Miss Sansom were to be dispensed with and it caused her to breathe even more fire and bile than usual.

Arnold was still thinking with amusement about Miss Sansom's dark-visaged fury on being banished from what she saw as a location of power, when he became aware of Detective Chief Inspector Culpeper walking ahead of him in the corridor, towards Arnold's room. When Culpeper tapped on his door, Arnold called out from behind him.

Culpeper turned. 'Ah, Landon, there you are. Could I have a word?'

Arnold nodded and led him into the office. They had come across each other on several occasions in the past, and while he felt they held each other in a degree of respect, there was no great liking between the two men. 'What can I do for you?' he asked, gesturing to Culpeper to take a seat.

Culpeper settled himself into the chair with a grunt. 'I'm investigating the murder of Steven O'Hara.'

'I guessed as much.'

'He was employed as a consultant here — I gather the submission he's been working on is now in your hands.'

'That's right.' Arnold frowned. 'You want to see the draft? I can't imagine it'll be of any assistance to you.'

'Who knows?' Culpeper said. 'I'd like to take a look at it, anyway.'

Arnold fished in the drawer of his desk. 'This is the original,' he said, handing over a thick manila envelope. 'I've taken a copy. It's just a submission to the Lottery for funding — it outlines the work at the Stangrove site, and the potential it shows. I can't see it'll help you in your investigation.'

Culpeper accepted the envelope, and peered inside it cautiously. 'You knew O'Hara very well?'

'Hardly at all. When he was appointed I took him up to Stangrove, showed him around and so on. After that, I think the only time I saw him was at the SPA conference.'

'Hmmm . . .' Culpeper put the envelope on the desk and drummed lightly on it with the fingers of his left hand. 'You didn't know him very well . . . but do you think he'd have made a good director of the Department of Museums and Antiquities?'

There was a short silence as Arnold stared at him uncertainly. 'It's not for me to say. I didn't know enough about him. And there was no certainty about his appointment. I mean, his experience . . .'

'Was not extensive.' Culpeper shifted his bulk in the chair, settled into a more comfortable position. 'Did that thought upset you? The fact that he was to be shortlisted, in spite of his lack of experience?'

Arnold shrugged. 'Not particularly.'

'But you're a candidate.'

'I've no great interest in getting the job.'

'Whereas Miss Stannard has?'

Arnold was silent for a little while. At last, he said, 'You'll have to ask her about that.'

Culpeper smiled vaguely. Landon always had been a closemouthed individual. 'It's just that I was thinking . . . Miss Stannard, it was, who started this idea of getting a grant from Lottery funding, I'm told. But the task was taken away from her — given to an outsider. I imagine she wasn't too pleased about that. And then, when Brent-Ellis has his . . . unfortunate accident, she finds that this *outsider* is also to be put up against her — along with you, of course — for the post of director. If I know Miss Stannard, that would really make her see red.'

'As I've already said—'

'I must see Miss Stannard about that, yes . . .' Culpeper regarded him owlishly for a little while. 'You mentioned that you saw O'Hara at the conference. You were there all the time?'

'That's right. I booked in for the whole conference and stayed till the bitter end. There were some first-class papers—'

'That first evening, did you see O'Hara?'

'Of course. He was on the top table. I saw him there, and in the reception area earlier — and later, for a while, after the dinner was over.'

There was something about the words that caused a tingling in Culpeper's veins. He narrowed his eyes thoughtfully, watching the man at the other side of the desk. He knew Landon fairly well. The man found it difficult to lie he, guessed, or to prevaricate. 'Perhaps you'd like to tell me what you remember about that first evening, Mr Landon,' he suggested in a gentle tone.

Arnold shook his head vaguely. 'A noisy reception. People wandering around chattering. Renewing old acquaintances. Fair amount of drink consumed. A good dinner. Nothing really untoward, or exceptional.'

'When did the official guests leave?' Culpeper asked innocently.

'Shortly after dinner — that is, they went into the reception area again for a little while first, with Colin Norfolk looking after them. But the two councillors — Tremain and

Patrick they left more or less together. About eleven-thirty, I would have guessed. Alan Farmer — he owns Stangrove Hall — he stayed on, talking with Miss Stannard—'

'O'Hara was an official guest, but he hadn't arranged to leave with the two councillors?'

'I shouldn't think so. When they left, he was still in the reception area where they'd reopened the bar.'

'Who drove O'Hara to the dinner? There was no car found belonging to him.'

'I can't tell you. I understood he intended staying the night, however. I believe he was booked in, but just for the one night.'

'And when was the last time *you* saw him?' Culpeper asked quietly.

'About twelve, I think. He was leaving the room. I . . .' The hesitation was brief, but Culpeper caught the uncertainty. 'I don't know whether he was going to bed at that point.'

'Was he alone?' Culpeper asked quickly.

Landon hesitated again, then shook his head. 'No. There was a woman with him. They walked out of the room together, but I've no idea where they were going.'

'And the woman . . . did you know her?'

Arnold's face was gloomy. He nodded, reluctantly. 'He'd been spending time in the bar with Sheila Norfolk, secretary to the conference. They left the room together.'

'Sheila Norfolk . . .' Culpeper wrinkled his brow. 'Wasn't that the name of the woman who was caught in bed with Simon Brent-Ellis?'

He didn't need a reply. The answer was obvious from Arnold Landon's face. 'And what about the woman's husband?' Culpeper continued. 'Was he still present?'

Arnold grimaced and nodded. 'Yes. Colin Norfolk was still there when his wife left the room with O'Hara.'

Culpeper paused, watching Arnold carefully. 'Mrs Norfolk had already caused a scandal by going to bed with Simon Brent-Ellis. Unfortunate business . . . Did this man

Norfolk demonstrate any . . . ah . . . displeasure at the sight of his wife leaving with O'Hara?'

Arnold looked Culpeper straight in the eye. 'He was lost to my view at that point. And I wasn't paying too much attention anyway.'

And with that Culpeper had to be satisfied.

2

Arnold spent the next weekend at the Stangrove dig.

The atmosphere was tense, an air of gloom seemed to have descended upon the site. George Pym was preoccupied and had little to say for himself. Arnold caught him casting worried glances from time to time in the direction of Sue Lawrence, who seemed withdrawn, her face pale, hugging private anxieties to herself.

Paul Samuels made no appearance at the dig for several days, but Arnold worked away with two assistants on the second of the three graves while George Pym continued his assessment of the shaman's tomb. The excavator stripped the topsoil swiftly, so they were able to move down to the required depth, calculated from their work on the previous grave site. It was not long before they began to come across signs that they were indeed working on a tomb site, and one of rich significance. Arnold slowed the work, ensuring that everything was fully marked out, taped, logged, as the first of the grave goods began to emerge from the dark earth.

A flagon and decorated bowl were the first items that caught their attention, to be teased from the earth with great care, and then bones were discovered. Arnold realized they were not human, but pig bones, left in the grave as a feast for the person travelling to the underworld. The others came across to inspect them. Sue Lawrence brightening up somewhat, and George Pym forgetting his own anxieties about her as together they crouched over the finds. It was quickly agreed that all should concentrate now on the site where Arnold was working, so the rest of the team came across to be assigned tasks on the new grave, which promised to be the tomb of a person of consequence. As the weekend progressed, their work was soon rewarded. A gaming board, the wood of which had rotted away, but which was still discernible by the metal corner pieces, with bone gaming counters lying close by; the head of a hand axe of a prodigious size, forged to be swung in battle; the metal clasps of a belt and scabbard, the leather long since worn away; and a stone, four-claw-footed animal figurine, with the face of an eagle and the breasts of a woman. It was evidence of a cult they had never come across before, and they were puzzled, but exhilarated.

Then, finally, they scraped in the ancient earth to bring to light the skeleton.

It was hunched, doubled up with a spearhead beside the left hand, decapitated, with the skull placed near the right hip and the lower jaw removed. The bones of the right arm were broken, and the chest cavity was damaged, possibly before death. To one side of the skeleton they found the bones of two dogs — one complete, the other dismembered. The man in the tomb had been tall, well-proportioned, and he had not been a young man when he died but it was clear that his life had been one of violence and death. The elaborate nature of the ritual that had been carried out suggested great anxiety that the dead man should reach the underworld.

The removal of the head, pointing to the underworld, would suggest a special ritual need for this man to have attained the kingdom of the plutonic deities below. I think what we have here,' George Pym suggested as they crouched over the ancient bones, 'is the remains of a great warrior, or even a king in his time . . .'

They took great care sifting through the tomb, Sue Lawrence taking sets of photographs as the grave goods were tagged and carried away to the hut for closer inspection, after their situation had been duly recorded and marked. That evening they stayed late at the site, excitedly discussing their finds, and the mood was lighter, the shadow cast over the group by the death of O'Hara lifted for a while.

The following morning Paul Samuels returned to the site.

He appeared somewhat disgruntled that he had not been present when they had opened up what they were now calling the Warrior's Grave. But he cheered up to a certain degree when he saw the grave goods, and pored over them enthusiastically, with Arnold, while the others continued their work at the grave site itself.

'This whole area is of great significance, I'm sure,' Samuels said enthusiastically. 'If we can only get the funding now to complete the work on site I'm sure we'll be able to prove the existence of an entirely new cult.'

'The submission will be going in shortly,' Arnold replied. 'I just have to agree a few changes with Karen Stannard, and then we'll see what response we get.'

Samuels nodded. 'We'll need that Lottery-funding support for the full investigation, and then there's the writing up of the find . . .' He glanced at Arnold. 'O'Hara did a reasonable job on the submission?'

'A very good one, in fact.'

Samuels grunted grudgingly. 'So the bastard did something right in the end.' He hesitated, scratched at his short-cropped hair and looked at Arnold with an air of uncertainty. 'You know I didn't like him . . . that there was trouble between us.'

'That was pretty obvious.'

Samuels scowled. He rarely shaved on site, and the dark stubble of his beard gave him a fierce, belligerent appearance. 'He came to see me at York, when I was working on my thesis. It was almost finished, and I had the intention of publishing in a few months. He was doing research for a series of articles on Roman York and he questioned me fairly closely. Maybe I was careless — told him more than I should have done about my own, original work.' His features were mottled with an old, but still violent anger. 'Somehow or other he got his hands on a draft of my research. It was probably that old fool Bernard Hewlett — he was my supervisor, and though he denied it, I can't think how otherwise O'Hara got his hands on the papers. Anyway, within weeks he'd developed a TV script — I'll say this, the bastard worked quickly — and sold it to a production company.' His mouth twisted as he thought back to it all. 'He ripped me off, trivialized my research. It was the wrong way to go about things. I had a learned paper in preparation, and it would have helped me to a chair in time. But he blew the whole damn thing for the chance to break into TV. Some of the issues raised were difficult to prove, and he made a mess of that. It set me back years. There's no way I could have produced my paper after he had written that damned script. But at least I prevented it from being shown.'

'The injunction?'

Samuels glanced at him in surprise. He nodded. 'You heard about it, then. Yes, I slapped an injunction on the production company. But I suppose it won't get heard now. With O'Hara dead, the whole thing goes up like a bubble. He was sticking things out, denying he'd used my notes. Alan Farmer no doubt will be relieved — I guess you know he's got an interest in the production company? And Bernard Hewlett will be happy. It gets him off the hook, because I'd complained to the university about his carelessness — which he denied, of course. It's still buggered up my research, but at least I have the satisfaction that the bastard got his comeuppance in the end.'

Curiously, Arnold asked, 'You'll be able to publish, surely, if the production company don't continue with the script—'

Samuels laughed shortly. 'Maybe so. I've lost heart, to tell you the truth. It was O'Hara who was digging his heels in. He'd been paid an advance, I believe, and insisted to the company that there was no plagiarism. They were reluctant, but going along with it, after spending so much money. But now they don't really want to continue — I've been seeing my lawyers and theirs the last couple of days, and I think we'll reach some kind of settlement.' He hesitated, took a deep breath. 'I've also been down to police headquarters at Ponteland. They interviewed me about that night at the hotel — the night O'Hara died. Have they talked to you?'

Arnold nodded. 'I've seen Culpeper.'

'I don't trust him. Hard case. Anyway, there wasn't much I could tell them. Went to bed early, myself. Didn't see anything of O'Hara after he left the top table.' He frowned, scratched the dark stubble of his chin. 'I was surprised when Alan Farmer swapped seats with him. I didn't think they were mates . . . Anyway, not much I could say to help the police. I had no reason to spend time with O'Hara that night — and that's one reason why I went early to bed. But I told them right out that I hated his guts. Culpeper seemed to think that was significant, but there's no way they can link me to the death of the bastard. He'll have to look elsewhere for the guy who clobbered O'Hara. Me, I'd like to shake his hand. The bastard had it coming . . .'

Arnold wondered to himself whether Samuels had expressed his dislike quite so strongly to DCI Culpeper. He shook his head. It was time that they concentrated on a death rather more remote from the present.

* * *

She was an attractive enough woman with a good body, Culpeper considered, though not exactly his type. He liked a woman with more flesh on her, like Margaret — who was built like a farmer's daughter should be. But Sheila Norfolk was good-looking enough, if somewhat pinched of features. Maybe that was the result of the pressures that had been building up on her of recent weeks. And she had bold, knowing, defiant eyes.

'You say you'd met O'Hara only briefly,' Culpeper suggested.

'That's right. I'd met him, was introduced to him before the conference, and then I spent some time with him at the conference itself.'

'In the bar.'

'With everyone else. It *was* a reception, you know.' She eyed Culpeper carefully. 'And he was sitting next to me on the top table at dinner. I don't quite know what happened, but Alan Farmer — who had been allocated the seat next to me — changed places with him.'

'You didn't mind?'

'Why should I?' There was a glint of malicious satisfaction in her eyes. 'It made my husband furious.'

'Why?'

'Ask him,' she replied with a self-satisfied, feline smile. 'Farmer went to sit near Karen Stannard, I understand.' Sheila Norfolk shrugged. 'I imagine that's why he did the swap. He's clearly attracted to her.'

'As you were attracted to Steven O'Hara?'

She was silent for a little while, regarding him with heavy-lidded eyes. Then the smile came back, slow, confident, mocking. 'Now who's been saying that? I found him . . . pleasant company. He talked to me in the bar, and we sat together at dinner — but that was accidental.'

'Nevertheless . . .'

She shrugged, with a studied indifference. 'He was an attractive man, a good conversationalist, he made me laugh. I knew most of the people at the conference, and they're largely a boring bunch. I've been attending the conferences for years, and it was interesting to see a new face, a man who wasn't afraid to enjoy himself.'

'That's why you stayed in his company, went to the bar with him after dinner?'

Her lip curled in grim amusement. 'Ah, I can imagine there'll be more than a few gossips who will have told you what they felt was going on.' She held his glance challengingly. 'Particularly after what happened with Simon Brent-Ellis.'

Culpeper was surprised that she had mentioned it. He toyed uncomfortably with the pencil on his desk. 'Brent-Ellis . . . yes. What exactly *did* happen there?'

Her eyes hardened. 'I don't see what it has to do with your enquiries into the death of O'Hara, but since I'm now branded as a scarlet woman I might as well tell you. Brent-Ellis had been running scared of his wife for years, but he'd always had a fancy for me. We'd met several times at these conferences, and he'd made it clear he was . . . interested. And, finally, I felt why the hell not?' There was a flash of defiance in her tone. 'There was no good reason why I shouldn't go to bed with him, even though I found him a boring, pompous fool. I had nothing better to do. And my husband had been doing the same thing for years, with various women.'

'And, unfortunately, Mrs Brent-Ellis found you together.'

'That,' Sheila Norfolk replied sarcastically, 'was not originally part of the plan.'

'I'm sure Brent-Ellis would be in agreement with that. But your . . . ah . . . fling with Brent-Ellis . . . did you have the same intention regarding O'Hara?'

She was silent for a little while, chewing at her lower lip .

She shook her head. 'I acted on impulse with Brent-Ellis. The end of it was . . . scary, I don't mind admitting. But then the attitudes everyone took up . . . expecting me to be sorry, repent, dig a hole for myself and hide, expecting me to stay away from the conference, branding me as a slut . . .' She glared bitterly at Culpeper. 'There was no criticism of my husband. Never has been, in spite of the way he's behaved over the years. So why should I be held up to gossip and what that stuffy bunch would call *contumely*? I threw it back in their teeth. I insisted on staying on as conference secretary. The whole thing would have collapsed without me, and they knew it. And I played up to their narrow-mindedness. I wasn't really interested in O'Hara, but since they thought

I was, I decided to defy them, strengthen and firm up their prejudices.'

'Is that why you left the bar with him?'

She shrugged indifferently.

'Where were you going?'

She sniffed. 'I don't know. He'd been drinking. He was . . . inclined to be amorous. He suggested we leave the bar and I suppose I thought we'd have gone to his room, but he said he needed some fresh air. We went out to the terrace . . . he grabbed me and he started fumbling away, but it was just a few minutes. He suddenly pulled back. It was as though he'd heard something . . . or remembered something. He got bloody rude then, suddenly, pushed me back into the hall. Told me to go to bed, said he'd be along later. And that's what I did. I must confess . . . I wondered whether he really would come up to me later. He never did.'

'You had a room separate from your husband?'

'That was *his* idea. After the Brent-Ellis incident.' She raised her head, challengingly. 'And that was all right with me.'

'What did O'Hara do when he pushed you back inside?'

She shook her head. 'As far as I could see, he was heading back out to the terrace.'

* * *

Later that morning, Culpeper was more able to understand her attitudes. He decided he did not like Colin Norfolk. The man was pompous, self-opinionated, and self-regarding. He was clearly angry with his wife, not least because of the stance she had taken after so many years of accepting her lot.

'I understand it was your idea you slept in separate rooms.'

Stiffly, Colin Norfolk said, 'She should not even have been at the conference. After that scandal at the sub-committee, when Brent-Ellis's wife caught them together and the man himself then died of a heart attack, she should have resigned, stayed away from the conference, not shown her face. But she was determined to make a fool of me — and an exhibition of herself.'

'You mean by drinking with O'Hara in the bar.'

'She was loud. She drew attention to herself.'

'Was that why you were angry that O'Hara was seated beside her at the top table?'

Colin Norfolk hesitated, his eyes wary. 'Who says I was angry? I was . . . concerned when I saw him sitting there. I didn't know O'Hara, he and Sheila had made an exhibition of themselves in the bar, and I was aware he had not been pencilled in for the top table. I approached them to check . . . maybe remonstrate would be a better word, because I thought she'd invited him there. But she told me, in no uncertain terms, I may add, that he was there by right, having made an arrangement with Alan Farmer. She was . . . noisy.'

'And you didn't like that,' Culpeper suggested complacently.

'Of course I didn't. She was my wife, and she was behaving badly with O'Hara — a virtual stranger. Everyone in the room was looking at her.'

'And at you.'

'Well, yes.' He wriggled uncomfortably in his chair, his handsome features pale with annoyance as he faced Culpeper across the desk. 'She was being indiscreet . . .'

'Unlike you.'

'What's that supposed to mean?' Norfolk bridled.

'I'm told you yourself have taken various opportunities at these conferences, and elsewhere. It's said you've had numerous affairs.'

'I don't see—'

'At least, that's what your wife says. She reckons that's why she jumped into bed with Simon Brent-Ellis . . . what's sauce for the goose, and so on. And then she got annoyed because people pointed the finger at her when you'd been doing the same thing for years without comment. And that's why she continued as she had decided to start — getting her own back. The thing is, you didn't like it.'

'I did not.'

'And you were angry.' Culpeper smiled thinly. 'The question is, were you angry enough to do something about it?'

'I don't know what you're suggesting!'

'You saw your wife leave the bar with O'Hara. What did you do then? Did you follow them? Did you see your wife leave him on the terrace? Is that when you had an argument? Is that when—'

'I had no argument with him! I didn't go to the terrace. I was still with my official guests. My duty—'

'It seems the official guests — Councillors Tremain and Patrick — had already gone. Your other guest — Alan Farmer — was in Karen Stannard's company. The fact is, others seem to suggest that shortly after O'Hara left the bar with your wife, you also left. Where did you go, Mr Norfolk?'

Norfolk's eyes were evasive. He was silent for a little while. Then he ducked his head, awkwardly. 'I . . . I did leave the bar to . . . to see what had happened to them. I went out to the lobby. I hung around for a bit, feeling foolish. They were on the terrace . . . I saw them. It was not a scene I could intrude upon.'

Culpeper's eyes widened. 'You saw them . . . and didn't intrude when you were about to be cuckolded again?' There was a short silence. Something happened to Norfolk's face: it seemed to lengthen in dismay, paling, and he licked his lips nervously. 'I . . . I had made my own arrangements.'

'You were going to visit another woman?'

Norfolk nodded reluctantly.

'Who was it?'

Norfolk grimaced, shook his head. 'It doesn't matter. Something went wrong. It just didn't happen. She didn't turn up where I expected her to. So . . . finally I went to bed.'

They deserved each other, Culpeper thought. But he didn't know whether to believe the man or not. 'So while your wife was canoodling with O'Hara on the terrace, you crept away to your own assignation?'

'It wasn't exactly an *assignation*,' Norfolk muttered. 'I sort of . . . expected the lady in question to be leaving the bar soon . . . I intended on casually meeting her on the stairs, near her room . . . but it just didn't happen.'

'So you can't actually prove where you were when O'Hara died.'

'Do I have to?' Norfolk almost squealed in concern. 'I mean, you don't really suspect that I could have killed that odious man?'

Blandly, Culpeper spread his hands wide. 'At this stage, Mr Norfolk, all we're doing is trying to fit together a jigsaw, taking witness statements, trying to find out what exactly happened that night — and who was the last person to see O'Hara alive.' He smiled. 'At the moment, that seems to have been you . . . apart from your wife, that is . . .'

He had enjoyed the sight of Colin Norfolk gasping and glaring like a terrified, stranded fish.

After Norfolk had gone, Culpeper began getting his notes into order for typing up. He was a careful, meticulous man in many ways, habits engrained in his early years as a copper on the beat when the paperwork had seemed endless. He cared for detail, and his reluctance to throwaway any old files he had been working on was legendary at headquarters. He had the theory that there could always be a time when information that seemed completely unimportant could yet result in producing a significant outcome. It wasn't a theory Farnsby subscribed to, but then, as a graduate he'd probably have an encyclopaedic memory, Culpeper snorted sarcastically to himself.

A conference of the investigation team had been called for later that morning and it was as well that Culpeper should be properly prepared for it. Young Farnsby would be leading the team through the progress reports and it wouldn't do for Culpeper to be shown wanting among junior officers. He was still at his notes when a call came through from reception. There was someone downstairs asking to see him.

A few minutes later Councillor Tom Patrick entered Culpeper's office. He accepted a seat but declined the offer of a coffee. Culpeper looked at the man curiously, he seemed nervous, and ill at ease. He had already been interviewed, along with Chief Executive Powell Frinton. Now he had chosen to pay a visit to headquarters of his own volition.

'I was on my way back from a breakfast meeting in Newcastle,' Patrick explained unconvincingly, 'and I thought it might be useful to call in. Have you . . . ah . . . have you made any progress since last we met?'

Culpeper made no reply for a little while. He checked back at the notes of his first interview with Tom Patrick. He'd detailed there the man's background, his business interests in the training agency he ran largely with government grants, his campaign for a seat on the council, and the results of the face-to-face interview in the presence of Powell Frinton. At last, in a stretched, uneasy silence, Culpeper folded his hands over his expanding waistline and leaned back in his chair. 'We're still talking to people. It's a long, slow task. Delegates from all over the country came to the conference where O'Hara died. They all need to be seen. So, we're . . . progressing, you might say.' He waited, as Patrick looked around the room, somewhat self-consciously. 'Have *you* anything more to tell me, Mr Patrick? Something that slipped your mind, when last we met?'

'Eh? Oh, no,' the councillor replied hastily, and then wrinkled his nose in doubt. 'No, it's not that . . . it's just that I, well, I thought I ought to come in for a chat. To clear up something.' He sat stiffly in the chair, almost to attention. 'You see, I wasn't exactly being terribly forthcoming. In front of the chief executive.'

Culpeper eyed the man curiously. 'In front of Mr Powell Frinton. Now why would that be?'

Tom Patrick could not meet Culpeper's eye. He looked down at his hands, linked the fingers, studied them, flicked some imaginary fluff from his cuffs. He took a deep breath. 'The fact is, I knew Steven O'Hara . . . knew him rather better than I'd sort of let on.'

Culpeper waited, allowing the jagged silence to grow around them. He cocked his head to one side, watching Tom

Patrick. The councillor grunted, deep in his chest. 'Look, I couldn't say this in front of Powell Frinton. He's such a bloody stickler for the rules. And O'Hara wanted . . . *needed* that consultancy job. So I . . .' His voice died away helplessly as he thrashed around mentally. 'I . . . I think I'd better start at the beginning.'

'It usually helps.'

Patrick inched his chair forward, leaned on the desk and managed a look of sincerity. 'You've got to understand, the job wasn't a fix . . . I really believe he was the right person to do the job. But the fact was, we sort of bent the rules a bit. I was chairing the committee that made the decision. The rules say that I'm supposed to declare an interest if I know the candidate. I didn't make the declaration. But I couldn't say that in front of Powell Frinton the other day. He's . . .'

'A stickler for the rules,' Culpeper supplied. 'So, you fiddled the consultancy job for O'Hara. But why would you do that?'

Patrick didn't like the word *fiddled* but accepted it wryly. He shook his head. 'I've known Steven O'Hara for about five years. You know I run a training firm, business management, that sort of thing. A considerable amount of the financial support we got was from the government — paying for places on training schemes. It meant I had to have in-house accountants. O'Hara was employed by me for about a year. It wasn't a big operation, he was qualified as an accountant, but not doing too well in private practice. Anyway, he worked for me for a while.' He broke off for a few moments, gazing reflectively out of the window. 'But the job didn't really suit him — he'd been doing freelance work for the newspapers, and when he finally picked up an offer he left. It suited his temperament better, journalism. Lord knows why he ever trained as an accountant in the first place. And then he seemed to strike it lucky. He got a freelance contract with a TV production company, to produce a script, until it blew up in his face. There were claims of plagiarism, suggestions he'd stolen some original research papers. That's when he came to me.'

Culpeper frowned. 'What did he want from you?'

Patrick exposed his teeth in a nervous grimace. 'We hadn't exactly kept in touch, but I'd come across him from time to time. And I quite liked him . . . he was a bit bouncy, but he was all right. Basically, he was asking me if I could do something for him. He needed money — asked me if I knew of anything going. That's when I told him that we were looking for a consultant to write a submission to the Lottery commission for funding. I knew it was the sort of thing he could do if he put his mind to it. And he did it well, too, as I knew he would,' he added defensively.

'You encouraged him to apply for the consultancy. And then sat in on his appointment without declaring your interest. Why would you do that?'

'I was sorry for him. We hadn't exactly been friends . . . but, well, I liked him, he was in difficulties over the injunction, I thought he needed the job, there were difficulties at the newspaper over the plagiarism thing and he was on the point of being sacked—'

'So you stuck your neck out.' Culpeper was suspicious, he felt there was something Patrick still hadn't explained. 'Tell me . . . do you know how O'Hara got to the conference dinner that night?'

Surprised by the sudden change in direction, Patrick raised his head, stared at Culpeper. He nodded. 'Yes. I drove him. He rang me, told me he was having trouble with his own car and asked if I could give him a lift.'

'But he was staying at the conference hotel, you were not. How was he going to get back?'

Patrick shrugged. 'I don't know. He said he was expecting to meet someone there, who'd be able to bring him back to Morpeth.'

'Where did you pick him up?'

'At his flat. He—'

'Did you go into the flat?'

Patrick shook his head. 'No. He was waiting in the street. I was in a bit of a hurry — we were a little late. We got to the hotel in good time, as it happened.'

'So you don't know how he was to get back from the hotel — or who he was to meet there?' When Patrick shook his head again, Culpeper paused, then returned to the earlier discussion. 'I find it strange that you behaved in so . . . friendly a fashion to someone whom you knew only as a former employee. Or was there a closer friendship?'

Patrick managed an uneasy laugh. 'No, we weren't friends. It was merely that I felt . . . sorry for him.'

'From what I've heard from others,' Culpeper said drily, 'O'Hara was well able to look after himself. He was confident, maybe even brash—'

'Mr Culpeper,' Patrick interrupted firmly, 'some years ago I had a problem. Alcohol. I defeated it once I recognized it. Quietly. Discreetly. But it was hard. It's given me a sympathy for . . . others who have problems.'

'Are you saying O'Hara was an alcoholic?' Culpeper asked in disbelief.

'No.' Patrick fixed Culpeper with a clear, level glance. 'But he did have a problem. It's one that's common among the Chinese, I understand, as well as the Irish. He had an addiction . . . not alcohol, but gambling. I'd been through my own agonies years ago; I could feel some sympathy for the trouble O'Hara was in. Like alcoholism, an obsession with gambling is a disease. It seemed a . . . Christian thing to do, to help him out.'

'Christian indeed,' Culpeper snorted, 'when it meant you were breaking the rules to give him employment as a consultant. How was that going to help him get over his gambling?'

'It would help him get rid of some of his immediate debts,' Tom Patrick affirmed, his eyes fixed sincerely on Culpeper. 'I didn't see myself as his guardian angel — but I was sorry for him, and there was a way I could help.'

'And that was the end of it?'

'Of course.'

'What about his shortlisting as a candidate for Brent-Ellis's job? I got the impression from Powell Frinton that too many of the rules were being bent in favour of this man O'Hara.'

Tom Patrick looked away, considered his reply carefully. 'I was on the committee that made the decision to suggest that compromise. But . . . it was a committee decision. We were all impressed by the submission he'd written.'

'But the rules were broken. Again.'

Tom Patrick nodded stiffly. 'So Powell Frinton argues. But it was all, really, a matter of . . . humanity.'

3

Farnsby cleared his throat and stood in front of the small group of detectives who had been assembled in the conference room. Culpeper sat to one side of him, in charge and yet not in charge. He was watching Farnsby, slouching somewhat in his chair, but clearly ready to pounce on any errors Farnsby might make. Farnsby was aware of it, and was tense.

'What I want to do today is summarize just where we've got to so far in the O'Hara killing. I've gathered all the information that's come in to date from the Midlands, the Met and Wales, and I've had a preliminary check run through Interpol. The first thing to report is that as far as the delegates are concerned, from outside the area, well, they seem a pretty unexceptionable bunch. We've come up with nothing, in fact, that can be seen as important. Few of them even met O'Hara, though several have provided corroborating evidence of statements we've received locally, concerning his movements that evening, his behaviour, who he was with, and so on . . .'

He glanced at Culpeper, nervously. 'Local interviews have been carried out by the DCI, and certain other leads have been followed up by others here in the room. We're able now to make an educated guess about the events — even though we have yet to receive full forensic reports. What seems to have happened is that O'Hara left his flat, was picked up by Councillor Patrick and driven to the conference. He spent time at the reception, went in to dinner on the top table, after switching seats with Alan Farmer, and then went back into the bar. Later that evening he was seen to leave the room with the woman he'd been dancing attendance on all evening — Mrs Norfolk. She tells us he went out on the terrace with her, then brought her back inside, before returning to the terrace. It looks as though that's where he was killed. He was then dragged out on to the golf course, hidden under the bushes where his body remained for four days. Sergeant Evans?'

The burly detective sergeant looked up and nodded. 'We've been around to his flat. There was no key found on O'Hara's body, but we gained entry by way of the landlord. We now think that during the period in which O'Hara's body lay undiscovered, the flat was entered — by using the key taken from his body — and a search was made of the premises. There was no great disturbance, but we think the place *was* turned over. We don't know what was being looked for. It could have been money.'

'Except that O'Hara didn't have any,' Culpeper interrupted.

'Yes, sir, I was coming to that,' Farnsby announced. 'We've checked O'Hara's bank accounts. He was skint. The DCI has come up with the information that O'Hara seems to have been a compulsive gambler and was probably under pressure to repay gambling debts. So far, we don't know who he owed money to — that's still being checked out. We *do* know he needed to take the consultancy job that was offered him because it would give him fees he could use to pay off some of his debts. But we don't know how large the debts were — or how much pressure he was under. Certainly, his journalistic colleagues have been unable to help — though they confirm that while he was with them, he gambled compulsively. Mainly the races.'

'So are we looking at a killing that was a reprisal for failing to pay gambling debts?' one of the group asked.

'Possibly. But why kill him, if he still owes money? It could have been a situation that got out of hand, of course. But we can't just home in on that possibility. We need to keep an open mind for the time being — there are others in the frame. Mr Culpeper — would you like to explain?'

Culpeper nodded ungraciously and lumbered to his feet. 'I've been conducting interviews with the locals who knew O'Hara. It's fair to say he wasn't one of the most popular characters around. First of all, he was involved in a dispute with a university lecturer called Paul Samuels. There's a claim of plagiarism — an injunction had been issued. Then there's a professor called Hewlett. He was involved in the same matter — and both men disliked O'Hara, maybe enough to get embroiled in an argument with him, and a blind striking-out.' He glanced at Farnsby, and added drily, 'Mr Farnsby did not, incidentally, touch upon the matter of the weapon — forensic have now confirmed that it was the object discovered at the scene of crime — a tyre jack handle. We haven't traced its owner yet.'

Farnsby's features were impassive as he stared at the audience.

'So Samuels and Hewlett are in the frame. We got the information about the gambling problem from Councillor Patrick, but he couldn't tell us the identity of the bookies involved. It was Patrick who got O'Hara his job as a consultant — and then, it seems, put O'Hara up for the job vacated by the death of Simon Brent-Ellis. Councillor Patrick seems to have been very supportive of O'Hara—' He paused, and scratched his cheek thoughtfully. 'He describes it as a Christian act. Trying to help an old acquaintance over a problem. I suppose it's in keeping with the image he projected to the voters, when he was elected to the council. Mr Christian Clean.'

He grunted, and shook his head, implying doubt. 'Anyway, by helping O'Hara, our councillor friend put two other noses out of joint. One belonged to Karen Stannard, at the moment deputy director of the Department of Museums and Antiquities, but expecting to follow in Brent-Ellis's footsteps. The other was her assistant, Arnold Landon, also shortlisted for the job. O'Hara had been shortlisted too, so they can't be discounted here.'

'So they're also in the frame?' Detective Sergeant Evans asked.

Culpeper paused, and looked around the room, frowning. 'Why not? At this stage, we look at everyone. Maybe it was one of the people I've mentioned; maybe it was someone else who bashed O'Hara with a tyre jack handle. The fact is, all of them were present at the conference the night he died.'

'Along with another two hundred people,' someone muttered.

'So do we concentrate just on the ones you mentioned, sir?' Detective Sergeant Evans asked.

Culpeper shook his head. 'No. O'Hara was unpopular in other directions too. The night he died he was . . . shall we say, somewhat active with one Sheila Norfolk. She reckons they started some shenanigans but then he broke away. Maybe that upset her, maybe *she* belted him. Certainly, she admits to having been with him on the terrace. On the other hand, her husband — who had already demonstrated a certain annoyance at the way his wife was behaving with O'Hara admits to having seen them together on the terrace. Both, of course, deny any involvement in his death. Both are unable to provide witnesses to where they were at the time of his demise. But things could have got out of hand . . . they could have acted independently, or in concert.' He humphed grumpily. 'But seeing O'Hara on the terrace, that's about the only thing they seem to have in common, apart from a dislike of each other.'

Culpeper paused, looking around the room, waiting for comments. When no one spoke, he went on, 'There's one other thing. When Patrick picked up O'Hara, he was told that O'Hara was expecting to meet someone at the conference who'd give him a lift back to Morpeth. Question is — who?'

There was a short silence. Farnsby glanced at Culpeper and raised his eyebrows.

'Yes?' Culpeper growled.

'I don't think we can discount the other official guest, sir. Alan Farmer.'

'How do you reckon he fits in?'

Farnsby hesitated. 'It's the matter of this plagiarism claim, sir. Farmer has an interest in the TV production company that entered a contract with O'Hara. Maybe it was *he* O'Hara had an appointment with. Maybe he tried to persuade O'Hara to back down from the contract — it was becoming embarrassing—'

'Too thin, Farnsby,' Culpeper growled in dismissive contempt.

Uncharacteristically, Farnsby bristled. Maybe his position as liaison officer was giving him ideas above his station. He glared at Culpeper. 'We need to remain *objective*, sir, and look at all possibilities.'

The tension between them was electric and there was a general silence in the room; finally Culpeper, scowling at the younger man, slowly sat down. He was not feeling too well suddenly, out of sorts, an odd pain in his arm. This was not the time to get into an argument with Farnsby. Let the young copper make a bloody fool of himself, he was the coordinator in this investigation. The game was getting too enervating for an ageing copper like himself. Maybe it was time to retire. The Farne Islands beckoned, invitingly, and he could almost smell the sea breezes . . .

* * *

Karen Stannard entered Arnold's room and stood leaning against the doorjamb with the file she had received from Arnold in her hand. She tapped it with an elegantly manicured fingernail. 'I've now gone through this submission, and it's all but ready. I've just been talking to the chairman of the committee. They've decided they want to make a bit of a splash about it all.'

'In what way?' Arnold asked, surprised.

'What would you expect?' She smiled, showing her perfect teeth. 'A press conference, a launch by way of a reception, where everyone who's had nothing to do with the project can come along and bask in reflected glory. Together with the workers, of course. I'll be there, naturally. I've also arranged for you to be present.'

In case there were any awkward questions, no doubt. Arnold grimaced. 'When is this . . . affair to be held?'

'Saturday next. The committee has decided that we'll also be inviting local groups with interests in archaeological matters. Including senior people from the Society of Professional Archaeologists.'

Arnold wondered whether that was wise, in view of the recent events at the conference, but kept his own counsel.

'So, make a note in your social diary,' she commented ironically. 'Meanwhile . . . as far as the submission is concerned I have some small queries. There seem to be a couple of references missing — O'Hara had tucked some odd slips of paper into the file, annotated in his own hand as *See notes*. What notes are being referred to?'

Arnold frowned and shook his head. 'Notes? I don't know. You've got everything that was in the original file.'

'O'Hara did most of the work on the submission up at Stangrove Hall, of course. Did he leave any papers in the library there?'

'You want me to check, next time I'm up at the dig?'

'Do that,' she said crisply. 'And then there's this — it was tucked in the sleeve of the folder you gave me.' She paused, frowning. 'These papers — they aren't the original submission papers, are they?'

'No. I gave the originals to DCI Culpeper, under his instructions. But I took copies, of course, for our own purposes. So the papers you have are the copies . . . though this is the original folder that O'Hara used. I put the papers for

Culpeper in a new folder after I'd copied them — that's the one Culpeper has.'

'Well, this note was tucked in the sleeve pocket of the folder. I don't know what it means.'

She handed him a single sheet of paper. It was doodled upon heavily, the heading in O'Hara's hand — *Ghost Dancers* — being ringed and marked about by fantastic figures. The doodles were followed by a list of several names, and a few initials. Arnold considered it, casting his mind back. He had no recollection of seeing it before. If it had been tucked into the sleeve of the folder, he could quite easily have missed it. 'I can't say I noticed it . . . I must have missed it when I was copying the submission papers. And I have no idea what it means. Do you think it might be something to do with the shaman's tomb, at Stangrove? Maybe some theory O'Hara had come up with?'

'Ritual attached to the burial, you mean? Ghost dancers . . . Hmm . . . interesting. Well, anyway, you'd better check it out. If there's anything to it . . . if he picked up something that we could use, it could give us an interesting title for the project. *The Ghost Dancers.*'

Arnold shook his head doubtfully. 'George Pym's made no mention of such shamanistic rites as a possibility. O'Hara couldn't have found something himself. It would have had to come from someone at the dig. And George would be the only source. O'Hara wasn't on speaking terms with Paul Samuels, and Sue Lawrence also seemed to avoid him.'

She shrugged. 'Maybe he was indulging in journalistic flights of fancy. Anyway, check it out. And I've also been looking at the latest report you put on my desk yesterday about the Stangrove dig.'

'My report on the Warrior's Grave?'

She nodded. 'Interesting. I'd like to have been there, when you uncovered the site, but with the duties I've taken on since Brent-Ellis's death, I've been overwhelmed . . .' She paused, eyeing him slyly. 'It's not a job you'd like, you know.'

'I've never said I wanted it.'

Her smile was cynical, she remained unconvinced. 'I've not heard what they're going to do now that the third candidate has been . . . removed from the scene. Have you?'

Arnold shrugged. 'I've heard nothing. I would have expected you — as acting head — to be the first to be informed.'

'Yes,' she muttered grimly, 'but you never know around here.'

She was a very beautiful and a very suspicious woman.

Arnold was aware that Karen Stannard saw herself as operating in a man's world, and that she needed to be one step ahead of the opposition at all times if she was to survive — though survival in her vocabulary meant winning. She had not spoken to him at all about the death of O'Hara, but she would certainly have seen his killing as an easing of her passage towards the directorship of the department. 'You were saying something about the dig?' he reminded her.

She furrowed her brow. 'Yes . . . I think it'll help support our case if we include some of the details of the Warrior's Grave in the application. I'll attach a summary as an appendix. And then . . . I understand there's a third ditch and enclosure that might contain a grave.'

'That's right.'

'I've spoken to Alan Farmer. He's prepared to continue helping us with the excavation, if we decide to open up the third area. Do you think Pym will go along with that suggestion?'

Arnold shook his head doubtfully. 'We still have a great deal to do at the warrior grave. To open up another site immediately, before we've properly investigated the first two . . .'

She clucked an impatient tongue. 'We need to pack as much as we can into this Lottery application. We need the finance. O'Hara's submission is all right as far as it goes, but I think we should take the chance to open up the third grave, and I can then send in an appendix after the main papers have been submitted. It will also help with the reception launch. We're likely to get more press interest if we can talk about another new grave.'

'We don't know whether there'll be anything in the third enclosure,' Arnold warned.

She stared at him with green, thoughtful eyes. 'Think positively. You've always had luck, Landon.'

And you've always had gall, he thought. He could guess at another reason why she wanted an early opening of the third enclosure: the appendix to the submission would be sent in her name. It would stand her in good stead when it came to the interview for Brent-Ellis's job. This was a time when archaeological best practice would be sacrificed to the altar of ambition. He sighed. 'I'll have a chat with George Pym.'

She nodded, and turned as though to go, then hesitated in the doorway. 'You'd better shelve what other work you've got on hand. This is important. Get up there as soon as you can, talk to Pym, persuade him to press on with the work.' She paused, there was a faint uncertainty in her glance. 'By the way, what do you think of Alan Farmer?'

Arnold allowed his surprise to echo in his voice. 'Farmer? He's very supportive. More than one has a right to expect, in fact.'

'Yes . . .' She was struggling to find the right words, which was uncharacteristic of her. 'I . . . I wouldn't want the wrong impression to get around . . . that there's anything . . . personal between us. I mean, I spend time with him because he's important to the project. That is, he's become a friend of course, but . . .' The words died away as she suddenly seemed to become aware of the weakness she was showing. Her nostrils flared in annoyance and she frowned at him, then turned on her heel and marched down the corridor.

Arnold was amazed. Karen Stannard was a strong-minded woman. There had been occasions in the past when she had reacted under stress, lost the iron control she normally possessed, but he had never seen her as uncertain as she had been for that last few moments in the doorway to his office.

He did not regard himself as her confidant. In many ways he knew she regarded him as a rival, even though once or twice he had detected a hint of reluctant admiration and puzzlement in her assessment of him. But this latest reaction was new to him, and he was confounded by it.

She had felt the need to try to explain something about Alan Farmer. But why to him? It was a puzzle that returned, drifting into his mind to plague him for the rest of the day.

CHAPTER FIVE

1

The following day, Arnold took Karen Stannard at her word and set off for Stangrove and the archaeological dig.

It was a beautiful morning. The hot sun was burning off an early mist in the valleys and the fells were grey-green, the distant sea a shimmering blue. He enjoyed the drive. The road was surprisingly quiet and through the open window he could catch the occasional tang of sea air as he drove closer to the coast.

When he arrived at the site, George Pym and Paul Samuels were already there at the hut, poring over some of the artefacts that had been discovered in the warrior grave. Arnold immediately suggested they have a conference to discuss the way forward at the dig.

'The fact is,' Arnold explained, 'Miss Stannard wants us to leave the work on the warrior grave for the time being, so that we can start on the third enclosure. She wants to strengthen the case for Lottery funding — if we can support the submission with reference to artefacts from the third enclosure it would help considerably. And,' he added, 'there's to be a press launch of the submission itself. I think we'll all be expected to be present.'

George Pym groaned. He did not care for official functions.

He shook his head doubtfully. 'It's not the best way forward, Arnold. We've only just exposed the second tomb. There's a lot of classification and cataloguing to do there. We need to map it in relation to the whole site, and there's the cleaning of the artefacts themselves. To open up the third enclosure is somewhat premature. And spending time at a reception is not a sensible way to go forward — all right for politicians, maybe, but a hindrance for us. And if we get bad weather . . .' He sighed. 'It's just not scientific . . .'

'But it is political,' Paul Samuels said philosophically. 'I can see her point. We need the money and that means maybe we should play along with the way things are done.'

Arnold was inclined to agree with George Pym, but felt that Karen Stannard's plans were more or less now fixed. After some debate, Pym grudgingly came around to his view and the three men finally left the hut and walked along to the third enclosure, taking another look at it to determine how best the enterprise could be managed. The excavator supplied by Alan Farmer was still standing by, though the operator was not on site, and they paced out the length and breadth of the enclosure, considering alternative methods of dealing with it. At last, George Pym shrugged and finally gave in. 'I suppose we'll have to go along with what our paymasters want — though it leaves me uneasy. It's not the way I'd like to proceed. I'll give Alan Farmer a call and get the driver to come up to the site.'

While Pym and Samuels went back to the hut, Arnold made his way to the Warrior's Grave. The young assistants were still at work there, carefully clearing the site, scraping, brushing and sifting for more evidence of the ritual burial that had been exposed. Arnold stood there watching them, contemplating the lives of those far-off, distant people. They would have had a close affinity to the supernatural. It would have ruled their lives. They would have believed that the air and darkness were inhabited by wild, fierce gods; that malevolent spirits stalked the land, demanding appeasement; and that a ritual burial for the great among them would be the only way to look to their futures as well as their past. The Stangrove team had discovered the tomb of a shaman and now a warrior. Arnold was fascinated by the thought of what they might find in the third enclosure. There would be a reason for their linking, but he suspected that whatever they found in the third tomb — if there was a tomb at all — the team would never really know the reason for their juxtaposition on the ridge above the ancient lagoons.

They would be able to make educated guesses, of course, when they had had time to consider their finds, discuss it amongst themselves, consult acknowledged experts in the field. But there were suggestions already that the cult they were exposing here seemed to have no counterpart elsewhere. It could make a good press story, of course, and if there *was* something in the tomb Karen Stannard might get her press interest yet . . .

George Pym came trudging up to him. 'Paul will stay on at the hut, working on the artefacts we've found so far in the warrior grave. The driver should be up here before midday to strip off the topsoil. Meanwhile, I think we could be usefully employed by taking measurements of the enclosure before he starts work.' He hesitated, glancing at Arnold. 'When exactly is this reception of Karen Stannard's?'

'Saturday next.'

George Pym swore. He folded his arms and shook his head in despair. 'That doesn't leave us much time. If we're going to turn up anything new, we'll have to get our skates on. It'll mean abandoning the other two enclosures completely for the time being. What a way to organize a dig . . .'

Arnold nodded in sympathy. 'I know what you mean. It's not the way I would have preferred to work, but I suppose if it helps the submission for funding . . . By the way, what's happened to Sue? I haven't seen her here at the site this morning.'

'She told me she'd be along later — or maybe tomorrow.' George Pym paused. He was hesitant, clearly worried about something as he glanced, frowning, at Arnold. 'Sue's not . . . she's not been herself lately. I don't know what it's all about but . . . she's become rather withdrawn. It seems to me she's not very well.'

'What's the trouble?'

Pym shrugged. 'I don't know. I've asked her if I can help, but she's disinclined to talk to me about it. But something's bothering her . . . in fact, my guess is she's been under a sort of stress for some time. And since O'Hara's death . . . well, I don't know.' He shuffled awkwardly. A big man, clumsily trying to hide his own anxieties. 'Maybe you could have a word with her. She might talk to you . . .'

Arnold was silent. He had long been aware that George Pym had a soft spot for Sue Lawrence. It was obvious from the way he looked at her from time to time, the protective manner in which he behaved towards her. He was a widower, Arnold gathered, and although Sue was a good ten years younger than he was, there was the possibility that Pym was hoping that a close relationship could develop. It was none of his business, of course, and he was prepared to talk to Sue if it would help, but he suspected she would talk to George if she would talk to anyone.

The excavator was brought into action that afternoon. It stripped the topsoil to a depth of eight inches, exposing the sandy soil beneath. They pegged out the area, dividing it into sections to which they could assign pairs of helpers, and reorganized the assistants on site. There were now eight of them, thanks to Alan Farmer's financial generosity. They began work immediately, scraping, sifting, removing stones, searching carefully for anything that might point to a burial. The other two enclosures had revealed their secrets at a depth of two feet but there could be no certainty that a similar pit-tomb would occur here. If there had been a burial, it might have been at a higher level. Arnold and George Pym agreed, however, that while the others sifted through the soil, it might be sensible to run a short trench in at one corner of the site to determine what might have been the relevant level.

They undertook it with care, and in the late afternoon they finally struck lucky: at a depth of eighteen inches they came across the edge of what appeared to be a stone slab. It was similar to those that had lain across the tombs in the other two enclosures, and it meant that it was likely that the third enclosure also contained a tomb, at roughly the same level, and slabbed in the same manner.

'Those ancient folk — they really believed that the spirits should not be allowed to escape again,' George Pym grunted, grinning with pleasure at the find. 'But this means we can work a bit faster. We'll run the trench inwards to the enclosure, along the level of the slab. It'll help us map out the area more clearly. We'll be able to locate the edges of the pit and work inwards from there.' He glanced about him at the darkening sky. 'But not tonight. The light will go shortly. We might as well call it a day and start again early in the morning. Have you checked in at the same hotel as us, Arnold?'

'I reserved a room by phone. Since Karen Stannard suggested I drop everything else and work up here for the time being, I thought I might as well join you for the rest of the week.'

'The extra pair of hands will be welcome . . . hands and eyes.' George Pym nodded. 'I'll stay on here and clear things up. I'll see you for dinner.'

Sue Lawrence joined the small group in the dining room that evening — the site assistants were being accommodated at a hostel nearby. The occasion was subdued. Samuels was intent on eating — he was a young man and he had a hearty appetite and he seemed particularly enamoured of the bottle of wine Arnold had ordered. Sue ate very little, but drank steadily, a second bottle of wine was called for. She spoke hardly at all. George Pym was preoccupied, concerned about her. After dinner, Samuels took his leave of them, muttering he had some reading to catch up on. George Pym suggested a nightcap and led Sue and Arnold into the bar. But he took one drink only, before leaving them. He gave Arnold a meaningful look as he walked away. It was clear he wanted to give Arnold the opportunity to have a private conversation with the female archaeologist.

'How long have you been working at the university, Sue?'

She toyed with her gin and tonic and shrugged. 'I guess it's just over five years now. The time's gone quickly. Most of it.'

'You've enjoyed the time there?'

She managed a smile, though it was weary at the edges. 'Contact with eager young minds is always stimulating. And practical experience like this dig also helps.'

Carefully, Arnold said, 'But you don't seem too happy at Stangrove, at the moment. Something bothering you?'

She frowned and was silent for a little while. Awkwardly, aware he might be trespassing on personal matters, Arnold added, 'It's just that . . . well, George is worried. He's concerned about you.'

'George is a very nice man.'

'And fond of you.'

'I like him too. But . . . well, that's all it is. At the moment, I'm somewhat lacking in a feeling of self-worth. And I wouldn't want George to . . .' She hesitated. 'It's clear you're aware he's got a sort of thing about me.'

'I've noticed.'

'He makes it pretty obvious,' she sighed. 'But I don't really want . . . I mean, I *like* him, but I can't think of him in the way I suspect he wants. But I don't want to hurt him . . .'

Arnold watched her silently. She was clearly not well. Her face was pale, and lines of stress were apparent around her mouth. Her eyes were shadowed, marked with anxiety. They had a haunted look about them, and she seemed thinner somehow, withdrawn into herself. As he looked at her she shivered suddenly, as though trying to pull herself out of some reverie. 'How are things going up at the site?' she asked, wanting to change the subject.

'We've had a change of plan. Or it's been changed for us. Instead of continuing work on the warrior grave we've decided to open up the third enclosure.'

'Why?'

'The need to secure more evidence, and quickly. To help the Lottery submission. And give some politicians the chance to get their pictures in the newspapers. There's to be a press conference and reception next Saturday.'

'You think the last enclosure will give us something?'

'It looks promising.' He hesitated. 'We missed you up there.'

'Yes. I'm sorry. It's just that I'm not feeling too bright lately.'

Arnold was silent for a little while, staring uncomfortably at the glass of lager George Pym had bought for him. 'Is there nothing I can do to help?'

She shook her head. 'It's just me, being stupid. There's nothing anyone can do really. It's all in the mind. It's like something that Steve said to me once . . . we're haunted, not by reality, but by those images we've put in place of reality. He was quoting someone else, of course. He never came up with anything original of his own,' she added bitterly.

'Steve?' Arnold queried.

She glanced at him, her eyes deep-hollowed. 'Steve O'Hara. The man who suddenly walked back into my life. Briefly.'

So that was it. Arnold recalled the day O'Hara had come up to the site. Sue Lawrence had been shaken then. There had been a brief altercation between Paul Samuels and O'Hara, but Sue also had shown that O'Hara's presence at Stangrove was unwelcome to her. Carefully, Arnold asked, 'You knew him well?'

She finished her drink with a sudden flourish and stood up. Her skin seemed hot and her hand was shaking slightly. 'You want another, Arnold?'

He felt she had already had enough to drink that evening. 'No, thanks. I'm fine. But—'

'No. I'll get it.'

He had interfered in matters that did not concern him. Gloomily, Arnold stared at his glass and waited for her to return. When she took her seat again, banging a large glass of gin down with a bottle of tonic, he spread his hands wide. 'Look, Sue, I'm sorry, it's none of my business—'

'Did you enjoy the conference?' she asked him abruptly. Taken aback, Arnold said, 'Well, yes, there were some interesting papers—'

'And what about the dinner, the first night?' she asked challengingly. 'Did you enjoy that, as well? Because I didn't. I hated every moment of it.'

Arnold stared at her, puzzled. Her eyes held a hint of wildness, a carelessness that had been brought on perhaps by alcohol, or maybe a high fever associated with her apparent illness. 'I can't say it was exactly my scene,' he replied carefully, 'but as dinners go—'

'I hated it,' she repeated. 'And you know why? Because I could see O'Hara for what he was, at last. And it made me realize how *stupid* I'd been.'

'I don't understand—'

'You asked me whether I knew Steve O'Hara well,' she interrupted. 'I knew him *very* well, in fact. I had just started at the university, in the Department of Archaeology, and had been there six months when I met him one night, in the university bar. God knows what he was doing there — I suspect now he was just looking for female company. But I was lonely, older than most other people there, and I found him attractive and amusing. He could be very charming, you know, in his Irish way. And he certainly charmed me.'

'Sue, I'm not sure—'

'We started an affair. He used to come to my rooms almost every other night. He had energy, and vitality, and I fell for him, hook, line and proverbial sinker. And then, quite suddenly, he dropped me. Cast me adrift, to continue with the nautical terminology.' She grimaced, contemptuous of herself. 'I was devastated. I couldn't understand why he did it. I'd thought he was in love with me. But it was all over — he dropped me when he got bored, just like that. I found it very difficult to come to terms with it all. We'd been so close. And then . . . nothing.'

There seemed no response Arnold could make.

'He'd recently got his job with the newspaper then — given up as an accountant. Wasn't a varied enough life for him, he said. Varied . . .' she sighed. 'One would have thought he'd make more money at accounting than journalism but it wasn't that . . . although he certainly spent money. Not so much on me, unless he had won a lot at the track. He was a gambler, you see. It was in his veins. But he enjoyed the newspaper work. He once told me — it gave him unparalleled opportunities to dig for dirt. Yet at the time, I didn't criticize him for that. I was . . . how do they put it? Wildly in love.' She glanced at Arnold, her mouth twisting in self-contempt. 'Do you think that's very stupid, Arnold?'

'I think it's a condition many people find themselves in.'

'But not you, Arnold. I bet, not you. Too cautious. Too careful. Too controlled.'

He wondered if that was true. Jane — the woman he was presently close to, emotionally, was in the States — they hadn't seen each other for some months. And he suspected they were drifting apart. Jane's calls had seemed cooler of late — more distant. But that was probably his fault, maybe he had never shown the degree of commitment she had desired. Too cautious, too controlled. Maybe Sue was right. 'Why did O'Hara break off the relationship?' he asked quietly.

'Because I was no longer of any use to him,' she replied coolly. 'You know, I used to smoke in those days. I wish I had a fag now. Ten a day was my mark. It was Steve who made me stop — so he was good for me in that respect at least.' She was using the words to cover her feelings, there were other things she really wanted to say.

'Catharsis,' she muttered, and picked up her drink, took a sip, grimaced and added some tonic to the gin. 'That's what old George probably had in mind, getting you to talk to me. Because he *did* ask you, didn't he? Transparent, is George. You don't need to deny it. Catharsis. He's a nice man, George, probably wants to be my lover, but after O'Hara I'm disinclined to get involved with anyone. You see, Arnold, the bastard used me, and I loathe myself for the way I went along with him. Especially since once I'd helped him, he dropped me.'

'How did he use you?' Arnold asked curiously.

'To betray a colleague,' she snapped angrily, but it was an anger directed at herself, not him.

'At the university?'

She glared at her glass and put it down carefully. She leaned back in her chair and regarded Arnold, inspected his features as though she was seeking some kind of reassurance. Then she sighed. 'I've kept it bottled up for so long, it's time I told someone. Maybe I should have told Paul long ago. It's been tough, working up here at Stangrove with him, and knowing how I'd behaved . . . At the university, it's been different, there was no reason why Paul and I should see much of each other — we work in different areas of the department, and we don't socialize particularly . . .'

'I don't understand. How is Paul involved? I take it you mean Paul Samuels?'

She nodded gloomily. 'That's right. Poor Paul. He got it wrong, you see, blaming Bernard Hewlett.'

Arnold was puzzled. It must have shown in his face for after a little while she smiled wearily and shook her head.

'Bernard was responsible for the supervision of various pieces of research in the department. Mine included. I had occasion to visit his study from time to time. And he rarely locked his room when he was in the lecture theatre. Anyway, there was one time when I went there in his absence, took some papers, and copied them. I replaced them later and Hewlett never missed them. He was always a bit slapdash in his filing — his room was always a mess.'

'The papers belonged to Paul Samuels?' Arnold asked, beginning to guess what was coming.

'That's right. You probably know the rest of the story. Paul was all set to publish, with Hewlett's name also appearing in the paper. But the gist of it was suddenly scripted as a TV production. By Steve O'Hara. There was an almighty row between Paul and Hewlett — Paul accused him of carelessness, even of jealousy, and then against Hewlett's advice Paul slapped an injunction on the production company.'

'But what was so important about the paper?' Arnold asked, puzzled. 'Surely — a piece of academic research—'

'You've never lived or worked in the academic environment,' Sue Lawrence interrupted cynically. 'It's like a hothouse. Professional jealousy abounds, everyone is out to produce original research, the number of university chairs are few, and Paul Samuels is ambitious. It was bad enough that Hewlett wanted to share some of the credit. When — as Paul thought — Hewlett was careless enough to blow Paul's chances of building a significant reputation that was hell for Paul. And the scripting . . . it trivialized his work. Emptied it of real significance. He went crazy. Oh, it was important enough to all concerned, believe me.' She gritted her teeth. 'Important enough to have me running scared. I kept my mouth shut during the ensuing row. It wasn't Hewlett to blame. It was me. And I kept quiet. Even after Steve O'Hara dumped me.'

Arnold was silent for a little while. 'I can hardly believe he entered a relationship with you merely to get at a piece of research.'

She smiled wearily. 'No, I guess not. There was something there at the beginning . . . But he used me nevertheless, and then dumped me. And I took it hard. That's why I was so shaken, when he walked into the hut at Stangrove. It all came back to me . . . not the guilt about Paul because that was with me all the time. Not that. It was the feeling . . . I remembered how it had been with O'Hara, at the beginning . . .' Her eyes misted over.

Arnold did not know what to say. They sat there without talking for several minutes. He finished his drink. 'You're depressed. Have you seen a doctor?' he asked gently.

'Prozac,' she smiled. 'That's what they come up with. The solution to all modern ills.'

'You've got to look forward, Sue, not back.'

'Easy to say. But to show you just how stupidly sentimental I am, even for a man who dumped me so brutally, you know what I did after I heard he was dead?' When

Arnold made no reply, she went on, 'I actually went down to Stangrove Hall and picked up the bits and pieces, the few files he'd left there in the library. As keepsakes. *Keepsakes*, for God's sake!'

She was close to tears, and not a little drunk. Arnold put out a hand, touched her arm. 'I think if you feel up to it, you should get back to work tomorrow. It'll take your mind off things. Go to bed now, get some sleep, and then come and join us when we work at the third enclosure tomorrow.'

She nodded. 'Forward, not back. Yeah, I get the message. Get down to some careful, practical work, keep my mind occupied, with you, and George . . . poor George.' She rose, a little unsteadily.

Arnold rose with her. He was struck by a sudden thought.

'Sue, you mentioned you'd picked up O'Hara's papers from the library at Stangrove. Did they include his working notes?'

She shrugged. 'I guess so. I haven't looked at them. Why?'

'Karen Stannard wants to check them. There's some reference to notes on ghost dancers. Maybe it's some theory he had about Stangrove . . .'

'Ghost dancers?' Sue Lawrence wrinkled her nose in thought. She shook her head. 'I don't know. I can let you have the papers, certainly. I have them here at the hotel. But ghost dancers . . .' She shook her head muzzily. 'Steve mentioned something like that to me once. He was laughing about something . . . was it the name of a horse he'd backed? Or what was it? I don't know — I'm too damn drunk now to remember, anyway. Maybe it'll come back in the morning.'

Arnold walked with her to the lift, escorted her to her room. 'I'll let you have the papers tomorrow, Arnold.' Suddenly, unexpectedly, she leaned forward and kissed him on the cheek. She stared at him for a few moments and then she came closer to him, kissed him again, on the lips. Her mouth was warm, moving softly under his and her body pressed close. Gently, he disengaged himself, held her slightly away from him by the shoulders, aware of the change in her breathing.

She leaned her head back against the door, smiling at him. 'The papers . . . you could, of course, come in and collect them now . . . although it would take a little time for me to find them . . .'

She was a lonely, disturbed and somewhat drunk young woman. There were rules about that sort of thing. Arnold smiled and shook his head. 'In the morning will do.'

Her smile faded and she observed him steadily. She nodded. 'You're a nice man, Arnold Landon. And so is George. I think I should have fallen in love with you, or with him, I guess, not that bastard O'Hara.' She heaved a theatrical sigh. Still . . . he stopped me smoking, after all. He told me it'd kill me. But I'm still here. And that bastard . . . he's the one who's dead.'

As she closed the door behind her, Arnold was suddenly struck by the aberrant edge of triumph in her tone.

2

They worked hard at the dig over the next few days.

It proved to be an exciting time. The team cleared the earth from the slabbed top of what they were convinced now was another tomb. The slabs were lifted with care and photographs taken of each event so that a full record was maintained. On the second day it became clear that it was indeed another pit and closely allied to the graves of the shaman and the warrior. Before they finally opened it and inspected the contents they discussed the matter in detail.

'There's every chance,' George Pym suggested, 'that what we have here is a group burial, the three graves being dug at the same time to accommodate some ritual deaths. We'll never be sure of the close link between the shaman and the warrior—'

'You think he might have been killed ritually, the same time as the warrior?' Arnold asked.

'It's unlikely, I would think. The shaman *may* have been killed to accompany the warrior to the underworld but I have my doubts: they were best at sniffing out other people for death. Even so, I guess it's a possibility. But I have a *feeling* about this third grave.'

'You think it really is also linked to the Warrior's Grave?' Paul Samuels asked.

'It's what my gut tells me — but we might never be sure.' He glanced at Sue Lawrence. 'What do you think?'

She seemed to have recovered somewhat after her rest away from the site or maybe it was the result of unburdening herself to Arnold. She was still pale, and her deep-set eyes were still shadowed, but returning to the site seemed to have helped her, brought a little more energy to her bearing. In response to George, she shrugged uncertainly. 'The artefacts in the shaman's grave are of the same period as those in the warrior grave so they're probably burials from the same period. Whether they were interred at the same time, who can tell? And as for this new tomb . . . you may well be right, George, but gut feelings are no substitute for hard research.'

George Pym laughed. '*Touché*. But even Arnold here admits to relying on instinct from time to time.'

Arnold was aware of the way in which Sue Lawrence barely glanced at him. He had the feeling she was slightly ashamed of her behaviour at the hotel, talking in personal terms with him, even though the conversation had been helpful in relieving her mind of some of her anxieties. 'Well, maybe we'll find something definite when we open the tomb this afternoon.'

When they left the hut to walk to the site Sue Lawrence detached herself from the others and walked beside Arnold. For a little while she said nothing, but then looked at him. 'I . . . er . . . I was a bit under the weather the other evening. Too much to drink, I guess.'

'Not enough that it was noticeable.'

'I'm not so sure about that,' she replied, grimacing. 'Anyway, I misled you somewhat.'

'Yes?'

'O'Hara's papers. I told you I'd collected them from Stangrove Hall and had them with me in the hotel. In fact, I was wrong. I did look for them this morning, before I came up here, but they weren't there. Then I remembered: I left them at my flat. But I can let you have them at the weekend. I'll be going home before the reception and I'll bring them back with me.'

'Don't worry about it,' Arnold reassured her. 'I doubt if there's anything of importance there. It's just that Karen Stannard wants to check the ghost-dancer reference, in case it's something O'Hara picked up which we missed. She wouldn't want to lose anything that would enhance the submission.'

'Hmm.' Sue Lawrence wrinkled her nose in thought. 'I don't think it really can be anything to do with the site, in fact. I've heard him use the phrase before we ever came to Stangrove. It was when he and I were still involved . . . I just can't remember the context.'

'If that is the case, it's unimportant. It'll come back to you . . . and Saturday will be early enough to have a look at it, in any case. Karen Stannard can wait.'

At the site they proceeded with care. It was a cool, overcast afternoon and the wind that came in from the sea beyond the ridge seemed to moan over the flatness of the ancient lagoons, while the blue-grey hills behind them gradually became shrouded with a creeping mist, as rain clouds built up in the west. They worked quietly, oddly subdued, eager to open the tomb before the predicted rains came and yet lacking the excitement they had earlier experienced. Arnold himself felt as though there was a brooding presence watching over them. He pushed the thought away as fanciful, but was aware at the same time that all of the group seemed to be tense and withdrawn as they worked silently at the slabs in the soft, sandy earth. After a while, George Pym suggested they take precautions against the weather by erecting a tent above the site. It proved to be sensible as a light drizzle began to descend. Their work was slowed as a consequence, and it was late afternoon before they managed to remove the last of the slabs and pick away at the debris that lay beneath it.

Their experience with the other two graves allowed them to work more quickly than they would otherwise have expected. There were certainly considerable similarities in the methods that had been used in the digging of all three tombs, and it was not long before Sue Lawrence let out a long hissing sound, suppressed excitement as she worked at the edge of the grave.

'Bones,' she said.

They worked beside her in the sandy soil to gradually uncover from the dust of centuries the outline of the complete skeleton of a man. The skull had been crushed, suggesting he had been pole-axed, but there were also the remains of fibres at the neck which suggested he might have been garrotted, additionally. He was unclothed, and there were no artefacts or weapons beside him, which suggested it had been a ritual killing.

Nor was he alone.

Beside him lay the skeleton which they quickly identified as that of a woman, huddled close, but what brought a cry almost of dismay from Sue Lawrence was the fact that a spearhead had been driven between them, effectively pinning their arms together in death. A cold, gloomy feeling grew upon them as they brushed the earth away from the bones. It was given voice by George Pym.

'I suspect there was no honour in this burial,' he said quietly.

As they worked, some of the enthusiasm they had earlier enjoyed was dissipated and an air of grimness descended upon all of them. Outside the confines of the shrouding tent there was a light, cold spattering of rain on the canvas and the wind was rising, whistling and moaning through the aperture that gave them light to work by. Any feelings of excitement they had earlier experienced slowly died in a silence that was broken only by the harshness of their breathing in the enclosed space and the keening sound of the wind outside. Arnold himself, felt a heaviness of heart. The find they had made was startling but its ramifications were depressing. Nor was its effect yet over. As he worked, scraping away near the pelvis of the female skeleton he suddenly felt a shiver run through him.

'Here,' Arnold said.

Sue Lawrence raised her head. She had been working close to the skull of the woman, while Paul Samuels and

George Pym had been cleaning the dirt away from the male skeleton 'What is it?' she asked, puzzled, staring at the tiny scatter of half-formed bone that Arnold pointed to.

It lay between the legs of the woman just below the pelvis.

'What is it?' she asked again. She edged forward, leaning over, staring. Then the breath hissed from her. 'Surely not—'

Arnold nodded sombrely.

'A *child*?' she asked.

'A child. Probably premature.'

'But . . .' She was silent for a little while, staring, and then she looked at Arnold with horror in her eyes. 'Are you suggesting . . .'

The words died away, and none of them spoke for a time. At last, Arnold nodded. 'It looks to me as though this was a ritualized, punitive killing. The man pole-axed and garrotted. The woman pinned to him with a spear through the arms. And these bones . . . It's a premature child. It was expelled from the womb . . . while the woman was unconscious.'

George Pym stood over them with arms limp at his sides, his brow creased. He glanced at Sue anxiously noting the trembling of her hands. 'The man . . . and the woman. Unconscious, you say?'

'The man was dead when he was interred,' Arnold suggested, 'but from the evidence we see, the child was expelled when the woman was unconscious, in the grave. Which means—'

Sue Lawrence gave a horrified gasp. 'She was pregnant and she was *buried alive!*'

* * *

DCI Culpeper was seated behind his desk enjoying a cup of afternoon tea when Farnsby tapped on the door and entered the room. He carried a thick file of papers and wore an expression of discontent. Culpeper was not displeased to see it. It was time Farnsby learned the hard way, that an investigation of this kind could be a long grind, even for a graduate copper who was the apple of the Chief Constable's eye. 'So, you *liaising* successfully?' he asked cuttingly.

'It's a nightmare,' Farnsby admitted, taking a seat in front of Culpeper's desk. Culpeper frowned at the impertinence but decided to say nothing.

'I've now got statements from just about everybody, and if there's one thing they have in common it's that no one admits to seeing anything that can be of much assistance to us. A number of people can confirm that O'Hara was dancing attendance on Sheila Norfolk that evening. Several commented that her husband wasn't too happy about that though a few were of the opinion he was only getting what he'd been giving her for years.'

'But the worm might have turned more than that,' Culpeper suggested.

Farnsby shrugged. 'That may be so. We have no confirmation that she went to bed when she said she did. And we don't have confirmation of her husband's movements either.'

'So he's still in our sights.'

'I suppose so.' Farnsby hesitated. 'Sheila Norfolk admits to being with O'Hara on the terrace — so had opportunity. But what motive?'

'Anger at rejection?' Culpeper suggested.

'I suppose it's possible . . . And Colin Norfolk had motive maybe — jealousy — but we can't fix him on the terrace with O'Hara. Though he can't prove what time he went to bed. On the other hand, his prints are certainly not to be lifted from the murder weapon — nor hers, in fact.'

'What about the other members of the merry band — the committee that the Norfolks ran?'

Farnsby shook his head doubtfully. 'Your report suggests Bernard Hewlett was waspish about the Norfolks, and bitter about O'Hara. There was no love lost between them — an argument about Hewlett's responsibility for papers written by Paul Samuels, and an injunction slapped on O'Hara and the TV company Alan Farmer has an interest in. It's all very intense, febrile even . . .'

Febrile? Culpeper grimaced.

'And though things can get a bit murderous, verbally speaking, in the kind of hothouse atmosphere these academics live in, it's still a far cry from one of them belting another with a tyre iron. Their attacks are more likely to be through articles in academic journals, or the courtroom.' Farnsby's features were mournful. 'There's just no way at the moment we can pin the killing on any of them.'

'The gambling angle?'

Farnsby nodded. 'We've interviewed three bookies. He certainly was in for significant amounts. But over the last few weeks he cleared off some of his debts—'

'Consultancy fees.'

'Could be. But there were also payments made, by way of lump sums, over the last couple of years. Whenever he got in *too* deep, he seemed to be able to find money from somewhere to pay the debts off. It wasn't cash that went through his bank accounts. So it's all a bit inconclusive. However . . .'

'Yes?'

'There is just one thing that emerged today.' Farnsby opened one of the files on his knee. 'I was going through the statements yet again, and a comment cropped up. It seemed a bit odd . . . so I followed it up with a phone call. You interviewed everyone local who was at the conference.'

'I did,' Culpeper agreed suspiciously.

'And none of them admitted to a, shall we say, *special* relationship with O'Hara?'

There was something prim about Farnsby on occasions. He seemed afraid to call a spade a bloody shovel. Culpeper scowled. 'By special you mean sexual?'

'That's right, sir,' Farnsby replied, sniffing slightly.

Culpeper shook his head. 'The only sexual bit comes out in O'Hara's relationship with Sheila Norfolk — and that, everyone seems to suggest, was probably not consummated. They weren't likely to have done it on the terrace.'

Farnsby licked his lips. 'There's one statement, from a professor at one of the universities down south who was at the conference — Gareth Robbins. He sort of hinted at a relationship between O'Hara and someone else who worked in the department.'

Culpeper glowered, thinking hard. 'There were several people . . . but only one woman as I recall—'

'Susan Lawrence,' Farnsby supplied. 'I followed up the hint. I was told that gossip at York suggests O'Hara had a fling with Miss Lawrence some time ago, and that she wasn't too happy when it broke up.'

Culpeper's eyes widened. 'I interviewed her, she had little to say — but she made no mention of a relationship with O'Hara. But are you suggesting she was badly cut up, so cut up by the end of an affair that she belted him with that tyre iron when she saw him with Sheila Norfolk?'

'Hell, fury, and woman scorned,' Farnsby said. 'Who's to say? But maybe we'd better have another word with her.'

'She didn't seem the type to me,' Culpeper observed, and then cursed inwardly as he saw the cynicism in Farnsby's eyes. It was the kind of statement that Culpeper would have jumped on, if Farnsby had made it.

'I think you should talk to her again. Sir.'

Culpeper made no secret of his displeasure at accepting it was his responsibility. He cast his mind back to his interview with Susan Lawrence. She said she'd gone to bed early that evening, after the dinner. She'd made no comment about knowing O'Hara. But had he pressed her on the matter on that occasion? Culpeper wriggled unhappily in his chair. 'I suppose so. I understand there's a reception — a press launch for their submission for a Lottery grant on Saturday evening, when a number of the local archaeologist clan will be present. Including the people we've been talking about. I think this is a matter for delicacy, Farnsby. I'll go along — and see if I can get something more out of the reluctant Miss Lawrence then. Meanwhile . . .'

'Yes, sir?'

'I'm sure you'll keep checking through the reports. Maybe you'll turn something else up. Late in the day.'

3

Holding the press conference and reception on the Saturday evening turned out to be a good idea. The prospect of free drinks and snacks ensured that there was a good attendance from the journalistic fraternity, and the local archaeologists also seemed to have appreciated the opportunity to re-gather in spite of — or perhaps because of — their meeting at the recent conference. Arnold suspected the whole event was successful in part because of the chance it gave them all to gossip, and get up to date with any news that might have been discovered with regard to the death of Steven O'Hara.

The discussion among the varied groups was already animated when Arnold arrived. He was a little late, most of the invited guests were already present when he entered the room in which the press conference was being held. He noted several councillors: Tremain, Tom Patrick, Selkirk, some members of the appropriate committees, and although he would have expected one of them to act as nominal controller of the occasion, he soon realized it was Karen Stannard who had taken it upon herself to act as hostess. She had commandeered the launch. There might be politicians present but she was clearly determined to attain the central position for the evening, and attract the limelight.

And she gleamed in it. Arnold thought he had never seen her look more beautiful. She was dressed in an elegant suit of pale blue; her hair and eyes shone. She flitted confidently among the invited guests, smiling, laughing, touching an arm here and there, making full use of her undeniable charisma. Nor was Arnold alone in his admiration. He noted how Alan Farmer's eyes followed her, and knew from his expression that if there had been any doubt about the man's feelings for her, they were indisputable now.

The wine flowed while they waited for the assembly to gather. It was clear that at the appropriate time statements would be made from the small raised stage at the far end of the room and as he edged among the gossiping throng, Arnold glimpsed a number of familiar faces. There were one or two men he knew among the journalists; Paul Samuels was there talking to a blonde girl Arnold did not recognize; Bernard Hewlett was holding court to a small group of seriously nodding acquaintances in one corner, waving his wine glass expansively; and George Pym was also present, big, clumsy, hovering as usual at Sue Lawrence's shoulder in a protective manner. Arnold was pleased to see she appeared to be more in control of herself now. Some of the pallor had gone, and she seemed to be quietly enjoying herself, chatting to some of her acquaintances from the earlier conference. As he moved along, Arnold noted that Sheila Norfolk had also turned up, defiantly; the animation of her gestures as she talked with some other female archaeologists seemed somewhat forced, and she kept her distance from her husband, her back firmly turned to him. Arnold vaguely wondered why they still remained together after the strains that must have developed in their relationship over the years. Colin Norfolk was clearly aware of her presence, casting glances in her direction from time to time as he maintained his position among a small group of men including members of his committee. It seemed she was still able to affect him by her behaviour on public occasions.

'Well, Arnold, all in position for the launch, hey?'

It was the young archaeologist Gareth Robbins. He clapped his hand on Arnold's shoulder and smiled, waving his glass to take in the whole chattering room. 'Quite a success, I'd say — the intellectuals meeting the press. And all in eager agreement. I imagine they'll all be saying to each other what an exciting time it's been recently in the world of archaeology. Sheila Norfolk jumping into bed with Simon Brent-Ellis to get her own back on her husband; Brent-Ellis dying of shock when his indignant wife burst in to expose his infidelity; the scandal of the defiant Sheila then trying to take on another man, only to have him getting his head bashed in with a tyre iron.' He grinned. 'She's not exactly a safe woman to know, don't you think? You might say she's become a bit of a femme fatale, hey?'

'They might on the other hand be talking about archaeological matters,' Arnold replied drily.

'Not if I know human nature. Though I will concede that there is great curiosity in that area too. I've heard rumours in the senior common room, of course, but little more. What exactly is it that you've been finding up at the Stangrove dig?'

'I think Karen Stannard is about to tell us all about it,' Arnold suggested.

She had moved up to the small stage, and the rostrum where a microphone had been placed. She switched it on. 'Ladies and gentlemen . . .' She smiled radiantly as the hubbub in the room died and the sound of clinking glasses faded respectfully away. 'I'm delighted that you've come in such numbers for the launch this evening. It is an important occasion and one which we hope will lead to great future success. It's not my intention to do much this evening other than give you an outline of what's been happening at the Stangrove dig, draw your attention to the information packs that are available at the table near the entrance to the room, and answer any questions you might have. And I should really begin by welcoming those members of the council who are here this evening, particularly Mr Tremain and Mr Patrick

— both of whom, incidentally, suggested I should speak at this meeting, as the professional involved, rather than one of them . . .'

There was a ripple of ironic applause from among the journalists and some of the archaeologists. Swiftly, she went on.

'. . . but I am the first to stress what great support they've given my department in the development of this project.'

'*My* department,' Gareth Robbins whispered in Arnold's ear. 'With poor Brent-Ellis barely cold in his grave!'

'I also give a particular welcome to those who have been personally involved in the dig — George Pym, the site director; Sue Lawrence and Paul Samuels from the university at York — it's their efforts which have given us this opportunity to be here together this evening — to mingle with the ladies and gentlemen of the press.'

'I thought *you'd* been working up at Stangrove as well, Arnold,' Robbins whispered caustically.

Arnold smiled. Gareth Robbins had failed to understand. Come hell or high water, this was going to be Karen Stannard's evening. She would take every opportunity to show people she was in charge in place of Brent-Ellis. She would hardly wish to draw attention to any of her rivals for the vacant post as head of the department.

She was talking about the early finds at Stangrove, describing the location and the importance of the site, and using an overhead projector to demonstrate the physical layout of the grave sites. It was all very slick and professional, Arnold thought.

'The first discovery of a grave on the ridge overlooking what in ancient times were lagoons proved to be important and exciting. It was a cremation, and gave some evidence that the site was a holy one, and probably used over generations, if not centuries. But the next discovery was even more exciting — a decapitated man, ritually laid out for his descent into the underworld. In your pack you'll find a description of the artefacts we found in what we're now designating as the Warrior's Grave. The team was, of course, stimulated by this important discovery, and with great support from the authority, and the generosity of Mr Alan Farmer, who owns the site, they proceeded apace thereafter. But it might be said they were unprepared for the next discovery, which may well be unique. A burial probably linked to the Warrior's Grave, of great ritual significance, involving the interment of a shaman.' She smiled around the gathering. 'While I'm sure you're all aware what a shaman is, if there are any of the uninitiated present, I'll suggest you think of medicine man, witch, warlock, doctor — a holy man—'

'There's nothing holy about the guy who operated on my big toe last week,' one of the journalists catcalled.

Against a ripple of laughter, his companion suggested, 'He was actually looking for his liver!'

Smiling, Karen Stannard waited for the noise to die down. 'I didn't know journalists still had livers . . . Anyway, it's against this background of the discovery of two ancient graves on a burial site of considerable antiquity — the warrior grave and the shaman grave — that we decided that in view of the importance of the finds, and the considerable cost of further work on the site we should make a submission to the Lottery Heritage Fund for financial support. A successful bid would enable us to continue the investigation, complete a report, establish a visitors centre and set up an exhibition of the artefacts from Stangrove. The submission was prepared in my department and it was to launch the presentation of the submission that this press conference—'

'And reception! Don't forget the booze!' the noisy journalist interrupted.

'Presentation, press conference, reception — and entertainment,' Karen Stannard replied, managing to smile edgily at the persistent interruption. 'It's all laid on this evening to launch our bid for financial support . . . And the exciting thing is, even as we were putting the final touches to the submission, further significant evidence has been exposed at Stangrove, emphasizing just how important the site is in our national heritage. This evening, I am able to announce that we have uncovered a third grave — one which surpasses even the others in its interest, in the light it casts upon our ancestors, with the story it seems to tell, the horror of the events that must have occurred millennia ago, the unveiling of a cult of terror that resulted in murder, and death and torture beyond even our sophisticated imagining . . .'

'My, my,' Gareth Robbins murmured, 'is it archaeology we're talking about here? The poetic touch. And she's to be your head of department, Arnold? With rhetoric like that I predict a glittering future for the department. She'll wind your political masters around her little finger.'

'She always has,' Arnold replied.

The questions came thick and fast from the journalists. From the information provided to her by Arnold, Karen Stannard had prepared herself well. She had produced sketch plans of the grave sites, the locations of the skeletons and artefacts, and even an artist's impression of what the final scene might have looked like at the latest grave site, on overhead projector slides which she flashed up for their edification. The artistic impression was a little too gorily romantic and lushly Victorian in style for Arnold's taste, but it went down well with the members of the press. She assured them copies of the sketches were available in their packs, and Arnold had no doubt the scene of the interment of the pregnant woman would be prominent in the newspapers over the next few days. Along with a shot of Karen Stannard, naturally.

She was, after all, rather more photogenic than any of the other people involved.

When the questions were over, all present were invited to continue to take advantage of the drinks available, and the planned light buffet was uncovered on the tables at the back of the room. Karen Stannard stepped down from the small stage and posed for a few photographs, some with the local authority councillors Tremain, Selkirk and Tom Patrick, others with George Pym and Alan Farmer. She was happy, and unable to contain her excitement. She began a progress that could be described almost as regal around the room. Arnold noted how Alan Farmer seemed to manage to remain at the fringe of the group that surrounded her, edging along at her side when she moved from one group to another. But the journalists finally drifted away towards the alcohol and the archaeologists towards the buffet, and small groups began to re-gather for usually desultory, sometimes animated, conversation.

It was then that Arnold saw Detective Chief Inspector Culpeper standing just inside the doorway. Surprised, Arnold watched him for a little while as he scanned the gathering, and then, as Arnold moved across to replenish his glass of red wine, he caught Culpeper's eye. The policeman nodded, smiling slightly, but made no move to come across to join him. Instead he continued his inspection of the room, as though he was seeking someone in the throng.

'I thought she was magnificent,' someone said at Arnold's shoulder.

Arnold turned, startled. It was Alan Farmer. The man's eyes were shining as he stood there with two empty glasses in his hands. 'The speech was brilliant. And the way she handled the journalists . . . but the content, didn't you think it was great? It was just the kind of launch the project needed. Marketing of this kind, it's essential, and she came across just right. You'll excuse me, Arnold? I just came over to get her a white wine.'

The man exchanged the glasses and then bustled away again, to join the small group talking with Karen Stannard. Arnold smiled. Although Alan Farmer was right in that she had handled it all quite perfectly, he felt that for Farmer, anything Karen Stannard did was perfection. He moved quietly along through the throng, looking for George Pym. He found him standing with Sue Lawrence, talking with the two councillors, Tremain and Patrick. He joined them, smiling at Sue, who rolled her eyes, clearly welcoming a friendly face in what was a stilted group.

'So the hard work is paying off,' Councillor Tremain was saying. 'It's good to see a local authority initiative enjoying such recognition. I've had a look at the submission myself, before the presentation this evening. It's a sound job. And if the money comes through, it will also help the case for further funding with the main council.'

'If the money comes through,' Arnold suggested, 'the council won't need to give it further support. It'll be Alan Farmer we'll have to thank.'

'Well, yes, of course,' Tremain blustered, 'but we were involved at the beginning, we've always given it significant support, and we wouldn't want to be seen to be pulling out at this stage. After all, it is a remarkable situation, the graves, the story they tell . . .'

And the fame could always redound to the credit of the councillors who had supported it, Arnold thought cynically. Not that Tremain had ever been a great supporter. He caught Tom Patrick's eye. The councillor smiled, possibly guessing what was in Arnold's mind. 'Well, we're not there yet, of course. The submission is good, I'm hopeful of the result. Karen Stannard's done a fine job.'

'It wasn't all her doing,' Sue Lawrence remarked, a little testily. 'Most of the work was done by Steven O'Hara.'

There was a short, embarrassed silence. It was clear that mention of the name was disturbing. They wanted no spectre at the feast of self-congratulation that was being enjoyed. Tom Patrick cleared his throat nervously, and shrugged. 'Well, yes, of course, O'Hara did the groundwork splendidly. But I think Karen has added finishing touches . . .' He appeared uneasy, not knowing what to say, unwilling to continue any discussion involving O'Hara. But he was drawn to it, nevertheless, in the well of silence that suddenly seemed to have engulfed the group. 'Has anyone . . . has anyone heard any more about the killing of the man? Have there been any further developments?'

'Not that I've heard,' George Pym said.

'You could always ask the man involved,' Arnold suggested.

'Involved in what?' Karen Stannard was joining them, Alan Farmer still in tow. He seemed tense, less at ease than when Arnold had spoken to him only minutes earlier, and there was a brittleness in Karen Stannard's voice that surprised Arnold. Suddenly, she seemed no longer to be enjoying herself. Her back was half turned to Farmer, and he shuffled beside her, unhappily.

'We're talking about the murder of O'Hara,' George Pym explained.

'On an evening like this?' Karen Stannard questioned.

'You yourself talked of death and torture, Miss Stannard,' Councillor Tremain remarked, grimacing uneasily.

'In antiquity — a few thousand years ago,' she retorted. 'But this is too close for comfort on what should be a triumphant occasion—'

'It's all of that,' Tom Patrick supplied. He hesitated, but was unable to restrain himself. 'But . . . I didn't understand what you meant, Landon, when you said—'

'Ask the man involved?' Arnold glanced around the room. 'I can't see him just at this moment, but DCI Culpeper is here.'

'The devil he is!' Karen Stannard snorted. 'He wasn't invited.'

'You can hardly throw him out,' Arnold observed. He looked at her, flushed and nervy, he was intrigued. This had been an evening of some success for Karen. Her presentation had been excellent and well received, the newspaper coverage was guaranteed by the sensationalism of the last find, congratulations had been showered on her and the publicity it produced would stand her in good stead for the post she was seeking. But she was on edge, irritated and uneasy; her eyes were restless and she was clearly concerned about something. She stared at him and her eyes were a dark blue-green, almost startling in their intensity. There was some kind of angry message in them, he had the impression momentarily that she wanted to talk to him, privately, but then the moment was gone, brushed aside as she turned to accept congratulations from Bernard Hewlett, Gareth Robbins and Colin Norfolk, wandering across to join them.

'We thought we should come over to offer our support, my dear, and our best wishes for the success of your submission.' Hewlett moved forward, edging Alan Farmer away imperceptibly as he took Karen Stannard's hand and bowed over it with an old-fashioned grace. 'I must say, Mr Tremain, Mr Patrick, you also should be congratulated. You have here an outstanding archaeologist working for you.'

'And a beautiful one,' Colin Norfolk added, not to be outdone in gallantry.

Suddenly, Arnold was at the edge of the group as they realigned themselves to accommodate Hewlett, Robbins and Norfolk. It had developed into a Karen Stannard admiration group, and Sue Lawrence also moved sideways, standing close to Arnold, away from George Pym's protective eye. As the others indulged in the process of congratulation and self-congratulation she leaned towards Arnold, muttering in a low voice, 'This is all getting a bit much for me. I'm going to duck out soon.'

'I shan't be too long myself.'

She hesitated and glanced nervously about her. 'You . . . you fancy a drink elsewhere?'

Arnold paused. He was not certain how to reply. He had no plans for the rest of the evening. He looked at the others — George Pym, Robbins, Tremain, Tom Patrick, Bernard Hewlett and a fatuously grinning Colin Norfolk, all hovering around Karen Stannard. 'What about George?'

Sue Lawrence sighed, lowering her eyes, whispering confidentially. 'I'm sorry to say this, but I'd really like a bit of a rest from George. It's . . . well, it's all getting a little overpowering, you know? He seems to have designated himself as my knight protector. I'd appreciate some other company for a while.'

Arnold nodded. 'All right. But I've not eaten, so rather than a drink, what do you think about dinner in town?'

'You're on.' She drained her glass.

'Will you tell George?'

She shook her head. 'No, I . . . er . . . I think I'll just make a vague announcement. And then, in due course we should just quietly make our way out. Separately, or George will only tag along.'

Arnold was a little uneasy at that. It seemed somewhat underhand, in view of George Pym's regard for her. 'Sue—'

'I know. I understand.' She grinned at him, mischievously. 'I'll be gentle with you. This is our first date. Dinner only. I'll make no untoward advances, I promise.'

He laughed at her archness. 'I didn't really mean—'

She shook her head, dismissing his protest. She turned, looking about her and suddenly raised her voice above the confidential whisper she had been employing. 'I'm going to get myself another drink, Arnold. You'll excuse me — you carry on here? Oh, and I've still got to get those papers of O'Hara's, you know, on the ghost dancers. I brought them with me as I promised — they're in my briefcase, in the car. I'll go and get them shortly . . . let you have them in a little while . . . And I've remembered the vague sort of context in which O'Hara spoke of them . . . he said the list was like a group of dancers, ghosting in and out. He said — now you see them, now you don't. So it wasn't really about the Stangrove site. Predated that, really. Anyway, I'll get the papers from the car shortly . . .'

The words came out in a momentary lull in the conversation within the group. Several heads turned to look at her as she detached herself and a sudden stillness fell. There was an odd feeling of isolation, as though they formed an island in a sea of conversation, swirling about them, and here there was nothing to be said. Arnold looked around him. Something had happened, or was happening. The conversation was stilled, a certain tension was apparent in the group. Next moment, as Sue Lawrence walked away and the group seemed to stand in shuffling, embarrassed silence, they saw Detective Chief Inspector Culpeper edging forward to intercept her, a glass of whisky in his hand. 'Miss Lawrence . . . may I have a quick word?'

As he led her away to one side, Karen Stannard broke an uneasy silence. 'I didn't think policemen drank on duty. Or maybe he's just here for the booze.'

Somehow it did nothing to lighten the air of tension. As though it disliked the proximity to the policeman, the group began to disintegrate. Colin Norfolk and Hewlett moving away, Tremain catching sight of someone he knew and Tom Patrick stepping aside also, with his hand on George Pym's arm. And in the short interval that followed they seemed to split away from one another, also, going their separate ways, as though each felt the other tainted by the presence of the policeman, or by something someone had said. Gareth Robbins murmured an apology and headed for the bar, and even Alan Farmer, after a moment, with a nervous mutter, ducked his head and offered to get Karen and Arnold another drink. When they both shook their heads, he moved away towards the bar to obtain another drink for himself.

Karen Stannard was alone with Arnold. She glared at him in displeasure as though he was responsible for the disappearance of her court. He was unaware of having said anything to upset her, but her eyes were bright with subdued annoyance. 'So what the hell am I supposed to do now?' she asked fiercely.

For a moment he thought she was referring to the disintegration of the admiring group. 'About what?'

'*Farmer*!' she hissed. 'He's given a lot already to the project, promised to support the submission, and bring in the TV company, and contact other businessmen in the North East to support the bid, so we can match the Lottery funding. Damn it — he's *essential* to the success of the bid!'

'So?' Arnold asked, bewildered.

'So the bloody fool's gone and asked me to marry him!'

When Alan Farmer returned to join them, Arnold, much to Karen Stannard's clear annoyance, took the opportunity to disengage himself. He was aware she wanted him to stay, but he was not in the business of protecting Karen Stannard from the consequences of her own behaviour. She had spent a great deal of time with Farmer, and no doubt allowed him to obtain a certain impression of her interest. Arnold knew she had been using his friendship to consolidate the support

Farmer was able to give to the Lottery submission, and she would have been well aware that he had been smitten by her. Now the pigeons were coming home to roost. He knew what was in her mind. Farmer was besotted with her and had now asked her to marry him. If she turned him down would his support for the project fade?

And if he did pull out of further support, she would be calculating what might then happen to her chances of succeeding Brent-Ellis as Director of the Department of Museums and Antiquities.

As Arnold moved away he saw the furious indecision in her eyes. It was directed at him, as though he were to blame for the predicament in which she found herself. But he was in no mood to help her. And he also was edgy suddenly, uneasy for a reason he could not pinpoint. Perhaps it was something to do with Sue Lawrence, he wondered what Culpeper wanted to talk to her about. Or maybe it was because of Karen Stannard. His own feelings about her had always been marked with ambivalence. She was infuriating and beautiful. She was bitchy and intelligent. He admired her professionally, but she distrusted him, regularly tried to undermine him, and they could hardly be called friends. Their relationship was prickly, professional and rarely personal. But she had the capacity to disturb him. And not least now, when Farmer had asked her to marry him.

Moodily, he moved around the room, having a word here and there with people he knew, sipping his wine. He wished Jane was here, back from the States. It had been a long time now since he had seen her . . . As he wandered aimlessly about the room, thinking dark thoughts, the noise about him grew as alcohol took its effect and voices were raised. But there had been a certain thinning already. Some of the people he knew had already left. He looked about him and saw Culpeper leaning against the far wall, alone, glass in hand, his glance fixed on the doorway.

Sue Lawrence was standing there, looking across to Arnold.

As he caught sight of her she smiled and lifted her chin. There was an edginess to her demeanour, maybe because she was fearful of attracting George Pym's attention, but she was clearly giving Arnold a signal, expecting him to follow, to keep their dinner date in town. Arnold drained his glass and replaced it on the bar. Culpeper was staring at him with curious eyes. Arnold nodded, and then threaded his way across the room. In the doorway, he looked back.

Karen Stannard was standing alone; Farmer was walking away from her towards the door, his mouth tight, his gait stiff, his back rigid with disappointment. Karen Stannard's face was pale and she was glaring at Arnold. He held her glance for a long moment, and then he turned, and left.

Outside, the night air was cool to his skin.

He stood there for a few seconds, aware that Farmer was walking past him, saying nothing, heading away into the darkness. It looked as though he had not got the answer from Karen Stannard that he might have expected. Arnold had no desire to meet him in the car park in the circumstances, so he waited for a short while before he began to make his way towards his own car. He had no idea where Sue Lawrence had left her vehicle, but he guessed she'd find some way of communicating with him, probably by waiting near the exit for him to appear in his own car.

The night was dark, and a cool wind had risen from the east. There was a hint of rain in the air and unaccountably Arnold's mind drifted back to Stangrove, and the events that must have occurred there millennia before. The artist's impression Karen Stannard had commissioned for her presentation was fanciful, but had contained elements of the reality that must have occurred: a dead man thrown into a grave, a struggling, pregnant woman held firmly, bound, perhaps speared through the arm already as they forced her into the tomb to drive the binding spear into his body also. She would have struggled, crying against the cruel hands, screaming to the gods to help her . . .

For a moment his skin crawled and the hairs rose at the nape of his neck as in his imagination he thought he heard her last desperate cries for help. He stopped, trembling, and then suddenly realized the cries were not in his head. A woman was screaming, in the dark parking area. Even as the realization came to him, he started running.

The cries came from the far edge of the car park, away from the lighted area near the hotel itself. As he ran, Arnold became aware of two dark figures, struggling near the perimeter fence, and then the cries were cut off abruptly as one of the figures was thrown aside, to fall to the ground. Arnold pounded forward, shouting. As he did so a car door was thrown open, the interior light flicked on and he could make out a man leaning forward, head and shoulders in the car, reaching into the dimly lit vehicle. Next moment he was dragging something out, and lurching away from the car, running and twisting between the parked cars, away to Arnold's left. Arnold shouted again but the man ignored him, as Arnold ran forward to see to the person lying on the ground.

He reached the car, breathing fast. The body on the ground was that of a woman, moaning. He leaned over her, touched her shoulder and she groaned, held her hand to her head, and shrank away, taking him for her assailant.

'It's all right, it's all right — he's gone,' he reassured her. She raised her head, and in the dim light from the car interior he recognized the woman who had been attacked. It was Sue Lawrence.

'Are you all right?'

She gasped, and nodded. 'He hit me . . . came up from behind when I unlocked the car door . . . I thought he was going to steal the car and I struggled, and he hit me . . . then I fell. Then he took something from the car. But I'm all right, it's mainly shock, I think. I'm shaking, but I'm all right—'

There was a confused shouting from the far end of the car park. Arnold hesitated, then lifted her to her feet, assisted her until she was sitting in the car. 'Don't move,' he warned her. 'Wait here, and I'll get help.'

She nodded, and he turned, heading towards the noise. There was some kind of struggle going on near one of the parked cars some fifty yards away, two men locked together, swaying, one of them shouting loudly. Arnold pounded towards the struggling figures. One of them seemed to be wielding something black and heavy, crashing it against the head of the man grappling with him, beating him down to his knees. As Arnold ran up, the man was still hanging on to the legs of his assailant, shouting for help, clinging to his knees as the dark, square object was raised again, clubbing, swinging down at the man's head. Next moment, Arnold was thudding into the man on his feet and they all went down in a tangled heap.

The man underneath him grunted, and clawed with one free hand at Arnold's face, scratching for his eyes, but Arnold heard a voice he recognized, 'Hold him, keep hold of him, for God's sake!'

It was Culpeper's voice. Wheezing, breathing harshly, the policeman rolled away from Arnold and the man struggling beneath him, and staggered to his feet. He leaned down, grabbing an arm, twisting it, and there was a cry of pain and frustration. Arnold rose groggily, glaring down at the man half kneeling on the ground.

'Now then, bonny lad,' Culpeper panted, his chest wheezing and rattling from his efforts. 'Just hold still, or I'll break your bloody arm.'

Someone else was running forward, joining them in the darkness, asking what was happening. Arnold recognized him; it was Alan Farmer. There was a groan of pain, and the man kneeling there with his arm locked in Culpeper's grip, looked up, grimacing at Arnold. His face was twisted, the breath ragged in his chest, his mouth contorted with fury. But even in the dim light Arnold realized who it was. It was the man who had appointed Steven O'Hara to write the submission for the Lottery bid: Councillor Tom Patrick.

'Hold still,' Culpeper snarled, 'and we'll get you back to the hotel. And then maybe we'll find out what's so important about that bloody briefcase you've been belting me with!'

4

'There's no way we'd have picked up the relevant information in our general investigation,' Farnsby announced gloomily. 'If it hadn't been for that slice of luck . . .'

Culpeper bridled somewhat. He snorted irritably. 'It
wasn't down to luck that I was at the press reception. It was
a good opportunity to observe, and question Sue Lawrence
— and it was she who had the important information, after
all. The information Tom Patrick had been looking for when
he turned over O'Hara's flat, after he killed him.'

The Chief Constable grunted. He seemed slightly put out
that it had been Culpeper and not Farnsby who had made the
arrest. 'And what exactly was the information she had?'

'It was a list of names, sir,' Farnsby said quickly before
Culpeper could respond. 'It all goes back to the time that
O'Hara worked as an accountant — before he turned to journalism. He spent a period in the employ of Tom Patrick,
and he had access to accounts relating to the grant payments
that Patrick was claiming from the Government Training
Agencies, in respect of young people who were on his training programmes. It seems the accounting checks carried
out by the agencies were somewhat loose and slapdash —
and Patrick had been putting fictitious names through for

grant payment — names of people who did not in fact exist. O'Hara picked up the fact that some of the names reappeared on various programmes but that the names and the training registers didn't match.'

'So where did Sue Lawrence come in?'

Culpeper intervened. 'Sue Lawrence had an affair with O'Hara at about that time. He had a loose mouth, it seems, and he was a boastful man. He gave her some hints about what he called his ghost dancers — they were names of people who danced in and out of Patrick's training accounts lists like ghosts. They didn't really exist. They were fictitious names Patrick added to his lists to make claims for government grants.'

'Are you telling me that at base this was all about a matter of petty fraud?' the Chief Constable glowered unbelievingly.

'Not so petty,' Culpeper replied. 'We're talking of a series of fraudulent transactions over a period of five years. Patrick obtained through his fraud something in excess of three hundred thousand — and O'Hara found out about it. After he left Patrick's employ, he made use of the knowledge.'

'He was blackmailing Patrick,' Farnsby added. 'O'Hara needed money to feed his gambling habit, and he screwed money out of the man who owned the training company claiming the spurious grants. That's why O'Hara was able to pay off debts from time to time with cash sums that never went through his bank accounts. Whenever he was in trouble, he got money out of Patrick.'

'Murder seems a somewhat extreme reaction,' the Chief Constable doubted.

Culpeper shrugged. 'You have to remember, Tom Patrick got his seat on the council on an anti-corruption ticket. Mr Clean, so to speak. He was still running his training business, but O'Hara kept popping up, asking for more money and threatening to expose him as a liar and a cheat if he didn't pay up. Kept telling him about his list of ghost dancers. It would have ruined Patrick's business and his reputation, if the fraud got out. In desperation, Tom Patrick kept paying him but there seemed no end to it. O'Hara continued to milk him. Then when he was on the point of losing his place with the newspaper, he pushed Patrick into giving him the lucrative consultancy job.'

'Which made Patrick particularly edgy,' Farnsby added. 'It was getting close to home — people were beginning to ask questions—'

'Such as the chief executive, Powell Frinton,' Culpeper said, glaring at Farnsby. 'But it still wasn't the end as far as O'Hara was concerned — when Brent-Ellis died, O'Hara saw the chance of a salaried post, which he regarded as a sinecure, in replacement of Brent-Ellis. But that, finally, was pushing too hard — Patrick was in danger of losing credibility, questions were being asked by Powell Frinton because proper appointment procedures weren't being followed, but O'Hara was still pressing him. And Patrick snapped.'

'That was the first night of the conference?' the Chief Constable asked.

Culpeper nodded. 'From what we can gather, Patrick picked O'Hara up at the flat, and as they drove to the conference told him he couldn't guarantee he'd get Brent-Ellis's job, even though he'd do what he could to help. O'Hara immediately asked him for more money. They quarrelled, Patrick refusing to help him further, but O'Hara insisted on pursuing the argument later. They arranged to meet after the dinner, on the terrace. But it was the end for Patrick. He left the hotel at the same time as Councillor Tremain, drove a short distance away and parked, then walked back to the hotel, for the meeting he'd arranged on the terrace. But he'd had enough — the demands were never-ending, Powell Frinton was asking questions, Patrick could lose everything if O'Hara opened his mouth, so he came prepared — with a tyre iron, from his car. We've checked that out — the equipment is missing from his vehicle. He waited for O'Hara to get rid of the Sheila Norfolk woman, then he joined him on the terrace — and hit him. O'Hara was drunk — didn't defend himself. One blow was enough.'

'And this Lawrence woman?'

'Patrick used O'Hara's keys to get into his flat after the killing — to see if he could find any reference, anything incriminating that O'Hara might have left around, but he found nothing. Sue Lawrence had heard O'Hara making reference to ghost dancers, without knowing what he was on about. And the list of names — which was all it was — had been left by O'Hara among working papers in the Stangrove Hall library. It really meant nothing to Sue Lawrence . . . but Karen Stannard had seen a reference to the list, Landon asked Sue Lawrence for it, and unhappily — or happily for us — she mentioned it when they were all at the press launch the other evening. She said that she had it in her car, and was going to give it to Landon. It would have meant nothing to them, but Tom Patrick was in the group nearby. He overheard her, knew exactly what was meant by *ghost dancers*, couldn't take the chance the list would fall into the hands of the police, realized it posed the danger of exposure for him and decided he'd have to get it from her. So he followed her into the car park — waited till she reached her car and then attacked her, grabbing the briefcase which contained O'Hara's list of fictitious claims.'

'Crazy,' the Chief Constable considered.

Culpeper nodded. 'Desperate. He'd come to the end of his tether. Battering O'Hara was in itself an act of desperation — he'd reached the end of the line. But if the names on the list were investigated — as they could well have been, although there must still be doubt whether it would have come to our attention — killing O'Hara would have been in vain — he would have been exposed. He had to take that last chance . . .'

'How did *you* come to be in the car park?' the Chief Constable enquired.

It was time for Farnsby to claim some credit. 'I'd got information,' he said quickly, 'that Sue Lawrence had been involved with O'Hara — something she hadn't told us—'

'So I went to the reception,' Culpeper interrupted smoothly, 'and spoke to Miss Lawrence, but she was disinclined to say much about O'Hara and her relationship with him. I was dissatisfied . . . and when I saw her leave, with Landon following, I was curious . . . I came out, to try to have another word with her. That's when I heard the commotion, saw Patrick running from her car with the briefcase, I tackled him. We were still struggling when Landon came up, and assisted me. It all ended up in a bit of a tangle . . .'

'The whole thing has been a tangle,' Farnsby observed gloomily.

Culpeper was not unhappy at his colleague's depressed state of mind. Farnsby had hoped to mastermind this whole business, to justify the Chief Constable's faith in him. Instead, Culpeper had almost stumbled on the truth. And stumble was the word, he was still aching from the struggle with Patrick in the car park. Maybe he was getting too old for the game. Time to retire. He glanced at the Chief Constable, who was staring at him with a coldness that made Culpeper wonder whether the same thought was in his mind. But the Chief Constable did not express it.

'Has Patrick admitted any of this?'

'He's made a statement. I don't think he'll give us much trouble. He's a shattered man,' Culpeper said.

'Well, this is not exactly an example of good police work, is it? I'm inclined to agree with Farnsby. It was all just a matter of luck, as much as anything else. Culminating in a scramble, in a car park. Not very *professional*.' The Chief Constable glared at them and pursed his lips unpleasantly. 'Get your reports in as soon as you can,' he said coldly, and dismissed them both.

* * *

'Ghost dancers,' Karen Stannard snapped contemptuously. 'When I saw the list in the first place, under that name, I assumed it was something to do with the Stangrove dig.'

Arnold shook his head. 'There's nothing to suggest it was so . . . there'd been no such references from George Pym.

200

O'Hara wasn't referring to shamanistic ritual. I gather from Culpeper it was just a list of names on training schemes, names of people who were non-existent.'

She was silent for a little while, but her glance was still locked on him, balefully. 'And you helped Culpeper arrest Tom Patrick. Who'd have believed it of him . . . ? What the hell were you doing out there in the car park, anyway?'

'I'd arranged to take Sue Lawrence to dinner. And she was going to give me the full list, to pass to you.'

'Is there something going on between you and the Lawrence woman?' she asked sharply.

Arnold was surprised. It was none of her business, his private life was nothing to do with her. Yet she was clearly annoyed about something in this connection. He held her glance. 'We're friends, that's all, from working together at Stangrove.'

He had done nothing to satisfy either her curiosity or assuage her annoyance. She tapped an irritated finger on the desk in front of her. 'Personal matters can get in the way of professional situations. An archaeological site is no place to conduct a romance.'

'There is no *romance*.'

'Yes, well . . .' She was aware she was treading on dangerous ground and she was annoyed as much with herself as with him. 'Anyway, with Patrick arrested, things have been thrown into turmoil with regard to the director's post. The whole thing's been delayed even further. Powell Frinton has told me I'll have to soldier on for a while, until they can get around to preparing a proper advertisement, and a suitable shortlist. That'll be your opportunity to withdraw your candidature, won't it?'

Arnold made no reply.

She stared at him, her eyes dark with a resentment that had nothing to do with the job, he guessed. He had annoyed her, and he could not be sure what the reason was. He wondered if it was something to do with her suspicions about Sue Lawrence.

'I don't know what Alan Farmer is going to do,' she said suddenly, changing the subject. 'He might withdraw his support for the dig. That could affect the Lottery submission.' She shook her head angrily. '*Men* . . . why can't they just . . . behave rationally?'

So she had turned him down, as Arnold thought she would.

She was staring at Arnold, and there was a confused air about her — he suspected it was a confusion brought about by thoughts of Alan Farmer, Sue Lawrence and herself. And perhaps her feelings towards Arnold — feelings she was unable to fathom, or comprehend. It was a puzzle to him, too. She regularly expressed and showed her dislike and mistrust of him, and yet she could get angry over a minor issue such as his planning to have dinner with Sue Lawrence. He sighed. She could be a mass of contradictions, on occasions.

Perhaps she herself thought so. She shook herself angrily, like a dog dispelling unwelcome rain water.

'When I *do* get this job, things will be changing around here.'

Arnold had no doubt about it.

EPILOGUE

The Old King was dying, but it was important that his honour remained intact.

The shamans had so advised, for otherwise his passage into the underworld would not be free and the bridge between this life and the next would be broken, and he would not come again. On his return from the long campaign it had been discovered that one of his young wives was with child. When it was known that she had, in the King's absence, lain with a youth the outcome was inevitable.

She had been his wife for three years and had remained barren. The young warrior she had taken to her bed was her own age, and the first signs that she was quick with child were already apparent. Where the Old King had failed, the youth had succeeded.

There were whispers that if the Old King had been capable of decision he might have spared the warrior — for the young man was a favoured spear-holder kept back at the village by injury during the campaign — and simply murdered the errant wife. But age and his injuries had affected his mind, and he lay drooling in the darkness of his hut, his mind reeling down the years, with wild incomprehensible words on his lips, a dying king communing with his gods.

Consequently, the decision was left to the shamans and they decreed that it was important that the wife and her lover were killed, in accordance with ritual, so that the Old King's soul would be free to join his ancestors in the world below, to cross the bridge, to shift his shape into that of another life, and to emerge again in time to lead the people once more.

So on the sacred cliff above the sea lagoons to the east they prepared the three tombs. The large one was lined with planks and the grave goods were prepared for the day — which could not now be too distant — when the Old King would be interred. Items of pottery were placed in the tomb, with wine jars, brooches, mirror, knives, and a sword, which would be ritually broken on the death of the King.

The second tomb was shallower. The shamans completed the rituals, they drugged the young man with the holy drinks and they stripped him. They sang their songs and scarred his torso with their long knives until the blood ran red down his body. He remained silent on his knees, drugged, stupefied, heedless of the pain and then they slipped the bowstring around his neck and tightened it, garrotting him slowly. Then, finally, as his body shuddered and jerked in the desperate search for air, they delivered the blow to his head that killed him. He lay in the dust while the dark air above him seemed to teem with shifting shapes under the wild keening of the shamans.

The woman was not drugged. Nor was she prepared to die quietly. She kicked and struggled as they bound her and screamed her defiant imprecations to the sky, until they stretched her body, writhing madly in the dust, beside that of the executed lover, and drove the spear head through their upper arms, binding them together in death as they had sought to be bound in life. She fainted then, from the pain in her arm, but they kept her alive, while they delivered their incantations to the gods. Then they lifted both man and woman, placed them side by side in the open grave and they filled her mouth with dirt.

The earth was thrown down on them as the shamans danced their ghost dance. And as the man and woman were buried, the onlookers saw the movement in the earth as she writhed in suffocation and the involuntary surging of her pelvis expelled the one who could not be king. He was not of the royal blood but would help serve in bondage to the Old King in the underworld, and the shamans chanted their songs to the darkening skies above the hill.

Then the people waited, and the shamans chanted and the darkness grew about them, but still the songs to the gods were sent skywards as the ritual fires flickered, keeping at bay the long shadows advancing from the dark trees. And in the morning it was time.

The old shaman who had entered the King's service two generations ago undertook the final rites. They gave the Old King scented drinks brewed from ancient herbs and he gasped, and his voice faded away while his breathing became stertorous and ragged. The shaman took the narrow, cylindrical rod with the fitted triangular blade and inserted it at the ritual point above the ear. The incision was deep, necessarily so that the inner strength that had served the Old King so well should escape, and be preserved in the dark air, until the Old King should come again. There was no cry from the dying man, lost in the stupor-inducing drug. And before dawn the cloth was placed over his face and his end came. They placed him in the pit and covered him with stones and the incantations were ended.

It was then time for the man who had served the Old King, so long and so well. The old shaman drank of the scented drinks and when he was deep in his trance they took the sharp-bladed knife and cut his throat so that the blood gushed blackly to the ground. He was buried in the third tomb. His medical instruments were placed by his side along with pottery dishes and cups and a Samian bowl. A wooden gaming board that had been his favourite pastime on earth was also interred with him.

All three tombs were covered with withy branches and earth and great stone slabs sealed with ritual. And after the two days of fasting and incantations to the gods the people were called to dig the enclosure ditches, for it was told to them by the shamans that the spirits of the dead were known to inhabit the tomb for some time after death, and the ditch was necessary to prevent those spirits escaping from the underworld and stalking the earth as malevolents . . .

THE END

ALSO BY ROY LEWIS

ERIC WARD MYSTERIES

INSPECTOR JOHN CROW

ARNOLD LANDON MYSTERIES

Thank you for reading this book.

If you enjoyed it please leave feedback on Amazon or Goodreads, and if there is anything we missed or you have a question about, then please get in touch. We appreciate you choosing our book.

Founded in 2014 in Shoreditch, London, we at Joffe Books pride ourselves on our history of innovative publishing. We were thrilled to be shortlisted for Independent Publisher of the Year at the British Book Awards.

www.joffebooks.com

We're very grateful to eagle-eyed readers who take the time to contact us. Please send any errors you find to corrections@joffebooks.com. We'll get them fixed ASAP.

Made in the USA
Monee, IL
08 September 2025

25248014R00125